DEATH IN SOHO

An Augusta Peel Mystery

EMILY ORGAN

Chapter 1

"OH, BOTHER!"

Augusta stooped down and gathered up the scattered pages from the linoleum floor. The spine of the book had ripped as she was taking it down from the shelf and the front cover had come off completely.

She arranged what remained of Thomas J Shepperton's *Collected Poems* on the table and sighed. The poor poet would be terribly disappointed if he could see the state of his book now.

Augusta angled her light and examined the pieces. The binding could be restitched, and the spine and cover would be straightforward to repair. Perhaps there was life in the *Collected Poems* yet. The volume was slim and the loose pages revealed Shepperton's fondness for singing shepherdesses, spring flowers and West Country sunsets.

All very pastoral, she thought. *What would he make of this chilly basement workshop on a plain shopping street in the heart of Bloomsbury?*

A knock sounded at the little window set high in the wall, and beyond it crouched Dorothy Jones at street-level.

Augusta could see only a pair of sturdy shoes, a green frock and a plump, waving hand, but she knew it was her friend. As Dorothy returned to full height and prepared to make her way down the steps, Augusta returned her attention to the book.

Why is the collection so slim? Were these the only poems worth collecting? Or is there a second volume? The book had been abandoned in the luggage rack of a train en route to Euston. *Had it been damaged by the repeated reading of an ardent fan?* There was no name fondly written inside the cover, stating anyone's claim to it. *Perhaps it was mis-mistreated by a reluctant scholar; knocked about in the satchel of a disgruntled schoolboy before being abruptly hurled onto the rack of a busy carriage, never to be studied again.*

The doorhandle turned and Dorothy stepped inside. "Oh, it's always so dingy in this place!" She rubbed her spectacles with a gloved finger, walked over to the work-bench and plonked her shopping basket down on it. "I don't know how you spend so much time down here. It's as if you're hiding away from the world!"

"Something like that."

"It's actually quite a nice day outside. Not bad for October, at least. I don't suppose you've been out much today." Dorothy pulled three books out of her basket. "These have seen better days. Mr Graham wants *Alf's Button* repaired quickly, as it's proving very popular at Holborn Library. We've two copies, but the other hasn't been returned on time. I've sent a letter to the borrower. I've also got *Great Expectations* here and *One Thousand and One Nights*." She paused as a low rumble made the walls and floor tremble. "There goes another tube train. We're between Russell Square and King's Cross here, aren't we?

Augusta nodded.

"Funny to think of all those people travelling beneath

2

our feet!" Dorothy continued. "I don't know how you put up with the noise. Anyway, let me know how long it'll take you to fix the books. I'll need to tell Mr Graham." She checked her watch. "Do we have time for a..."

"Cup of tea?"

"That would be lovely."

Augusta led the way up the steps to the street, wondering why Dorothy had chosen to work in a library when she liked to chat so much. They stepped through the door, which adjoined a tailor's shop, then up the three flights of stairs to her little flat on the top floor.

"You still have the budgerigar, I see," said Dorothy, stepping across the room to examine the yellow bird in its cage.

"*Canary*. And not just an ordinary canary; it's a prize-winning bird."

"What did it win?"

"Lady Hereford explained it once, but I can't recall the detail now."

"Goes on a bit, does she?"

"I think she gets lonely."

"Well, anyone would get a bit lonely living all on their own in a hotel. Especially a widow... I know all about that. Not that I live in a hotel, of course. It must cost an arm and a leg to stay there. She and her husband had that enormous estate before the war, didn't they? Life must have been quite different back then. Still, I suppose she's had plenty of people to talk to since she's been in hospital. A captive audience, I'd say. Hopefully she'll be out again soon so you can give the bird back. Doesn't the cage take up an awful lot of space? Very fancy, too! It's the same shape as the Taj Mahal. Actually, it's not the Taj Mahal; it's the Brighton Pavilion. Have you ever been there? It feels like you're in India. A little budgerigar in an enormous Indian palace!" She gave a low chuckle.

"*Canary.*"

"I haven't told you about Harriet's bit of excitement the other morning yet. She helped Lord Shellbrook after he crashed his car in Piccadilly Circus. Did you hear about it?"

"Harriet was there?"

"Yes, she was taking an early morning walk before breakfast. I don't know what she was doing down by Piccadilly Circus... perhaps she wanted to catch a glimpse of the statue of Eros. She certainly got more than she'd bargained for when she saw Lord Shellbrook plough directly into it! He was lucky someone happened to be close by and raised the alarm! Not that he was seriously hurt, anyway. I suspect the only real injury was to his pride. Besides, he was probably drunk. Speaking of Harriet, I have a favour to ask."

"Chaperone duties?"

"I'm afraid so. They intend to visit a restaurant on Wednesday. Do you mind? You really would be doing me the most enormous favour again. You know how I worry."

"Is it that theatre manager again?"

"Yes, Gabriel Lennox. I suppose I should be flattered he's taken such an interest in her, but it's placing a terrible strain on my nerves. I know all about the kind of flashy girls you find in the West End these days." Her brow creased. "And not just the West End; all over London. Loose morals, extravagant habits and..." she lowered her voice, "cocaine, too."

Augusta set the cups down in their saucers, listening silently as Dorothy chatted away.

"I know I shouldn't keep harking back to the tragic case of that actress, Billie Carleton, but I'm afraid I can't

4

help it. Dead at just twenty-two after taking that horrible stuff. Can you imagine if it happened to your daughter?"

"I can't imagine it happening to Harriet."

"Well, neither could I until a short while ago. But those dancers and actresses are just the sorts of people she's been carrying on with since she met Mr Lennox!"

"Harriet's a sewing mistress, not an actress or a dancer."

"There's still time." Dorothy shuddered. "And that's why I'm so old-fashioned and insist on her having a chaperone. She would never agree to me chaperoning her, and you're the only other lady of a certain age I trust. If my Christopher were still here…" She pursed her lips and drew a shaky breath in through her nose before recovering herself. "If my Christopher were still here, Harriet would behave properly."

"I've no doubt Harriet would be stepping out with Gabriel Lennox even if Christopher were still here. She's young, and London's an exciting place. Surely you wouldn't want her to grow old and sensible too quickly."

"I'd be perfectly happy if Harriet grew old and sensible right away! What's your opinion of Lennox? Do you think he's a good sort of chap?"

Augusta pictured the lascivious, red-haired braggart. *Hardly an ideal match for young, naive Harriet.* "I don't know him well enough to pass comment."

"What does your instinct tell you?"

"That the relationship will be short-lived."

"That's a relief, I suppose. He has some impressive accomplishments under his belt, mind you. It was his theatre that put on *The Maid From the Orient*. Did you know that it was the longest-running play in the West End?"

"Yes, I've heard all about it."

"It provided wonderful entertainment for all the

servicemen on leave from the front. Shows like that were just what we needed during those dark days."

Half an hour later, Augusta watched from her window as Dorothy's squat form bustled off down Marchmont Street.

"I want Harriet home by eleven," she'd said just before she left. "And whatever you do, don't let her go anywhere near those awful nightclubs."

Augusta noticed a man in a trench coat standing outside the draper's shop, his face hidden beneath the brim of his hat.

He seemed familiar somehow. He lit a cigarette, then looked up at her window.

Startled, Augusta stepped back.

It was *him*.

Surely he couldn't have found out where she lived...

Chapter 2

"DID you deliberately choose that outfit to match your eyes?" Gabriel Lennox asked Harriet Jones as they dined at a popular Soho restaurant. "Or was it just a happy accident?"

Augusta felt her toes curl as she pretended to read a book at her table by the wall.

Harriet giggled. "Oh, you're such a funny bear, Gabriel!"

"Quite seriously, though, you look astoundingly beautiful this evening." Gabriel was lounging in his chair, one arm hooked over its back. Hitching up the trouser leg of his well-tailored suit, he flung his right leg over the left and swung his elevated foot. "I reckon I'm the luckiest chap in this restaurant. What am I saying? I'm the luckiest chap in the whole of London town! I say, waiter!"

A white-jacketed man slid up to the table. "Yes, sir?"

"Don't you agree that my companion is the most beautiful lady in all of London?"

The waiter gave a bow, his expression impassive. "Of course. Very beautiful indeed, madam."

"Thank you!" she chimed as the waiter slipped away again. "Oh Gabriel, how embarrassing!"

Augusta suspected Harriet was rather flattered by the attention and not embarrassed at all.

"Just you wait. I shall declare it from the top of Nelson's Column before the evening is out!"

Harriet giggled again and Augusta checked her watch. Only ten minutes had passed since she last looked.

The waiter picked up Augusta's empty cup and saucer. "Can I get you anything else, madam?"

"Another tea, thank you."

"Perhaps madam would prefer something a little stronger?"

A glance at the polished brogue dangling from the toe of Gabriel's swinging foot was enough to persuade her. "A brandy, then. Thank you."

"Can you believe I was once an actor?" Gabriel asked Harriet.

"I can't imagine you on the stage."

"Can't imagine it? Why ever not?"

"Because I've never seen you do it."

"There are lots of things you haven't seen me do yet."

Harriet dissolved into abashed laughter, then busied herself with her cigarette case.

"Here, allow me." Gabriel leaned across the table, lighter in hand.

Harriet smiled as she held the cigarette holder between her painted lips.

Framed by the fronds of potted palms, the pair made a handsome couple. The beads in Harriet's headband glittered, and her dress was a shimmering peacock blue. Smoothing her dark, bobbed hair, she inhaled deeply on her cigarette before flashing a smile that appeared to mesmerise her companion. *She probably is the most beautiful girl in London*, Augusta reflected. She pictured plump Dorothy and wondered whether she had been nearly as attractive in her youth.

"My first starring role came about at the age of fourteen," declared Gabriel. "*A Midsummer Night's Dream*, it was. I played Puck. You're familiar with Puck, are you?"

"Yes, he's a funny character. Was comedy your forte?"

"I did a bit of everything, actually. Comedy, tragedy… you name it."

"Why did you stop?"

"I wanted to be the chap in charge. I'm rather bossy, you see."

"Oh, I can't imagine that."

"You're most beguiling when you're being sarcastic, Miss Jones." He slouched back in his chair and puffed a plume of smoke up at a chandelier. "You should come and see the new show, *An Evening Swansong*. The opening's been delayed a little, but I'll make sure you have the best seat in the house."

"The royal box?"

"Most definitely! You deserve it. I like you, Harri. You're different."

"Should I take that as a compliment?"

"Of course! You're quite different from any girl I've ever known before. You have a proper job, for one thing. The rest of us are simply playing at it."

"You mean people in the theatre business?"

"Absolutely! When you've been in the business as long as I have, you realise everyone's just playing a game. We provide entertainment, of course, but it's not nearly as important as teaching sewing to girls."

"Oh, I don't think that's so very important."

"You're a teacher!"

"Only a sewing mistress."

"It's still important. I should put on a play about a school at the Olympus, I reckon."

"That sounds terribly dull!"

"It needn't be; I have lots of ideas. I can already imagine how some of the songs would go. Would you come and see it if I did?"

"I'd come to all your plays, Gabriel."

Harriet left the table to powder her nose after the first course.

"Mrs Peel." Gabriel turned to face Augusta, ran a hand through his red hair and grinned. "Is that one of the books you've repaired?"

"No, just one I borrowed from the library."

"I never find the time to read myself; I'm always so busy. You, on the other hand, appear to spend most of your time surrounded by books. I suppose that's the life of a bookbinder for you."

"I'm not a professional bookbinder. I've never had any proper training, as such. I just repair books I feel sorry for."

"There must be a skill to it, though." He lit another cigarette. He looked at least ten years older than Harriet, possibly fifteen. Not a great deal younger than herself, in fact. She figured it was possible he had already been married, and perhaps there were even children on the scene. Augusta doubted he had told Harriet much about his past.

"I haven't had the pleasure of meeting Mrs Jones yet," he said. "What's she like?"

"Quite different from Harriet."

"How interesting. Is she a beauty?"

"You know what they say about beauty."

"That it's in the eye of the beholder?" He threw back his head and laughed. "Such a tactful response, Mrs Peel! I suppose I shall have to judge for myself, in that case. I should very much like to meet her. I'm quite taken with Harri, as you can probably tell."

"You be kind to her, Mr Lennox. She's a respectable girl from a good family."

His mouth dropped open in mock offence. "What do you take me for?"

"I know your type."

"I'd be interested to hear how you've come to know about men of *my type*, Mrs Peel."

"I'm not telling you."

He grinned, clearly enjoying this mild conflict. "I shall order you another brandy. Perhaps you'll tell me then."

"Harriet is your companion this evening, Mr Lennox, not me."

"I once knew a chap who eloped with his girl's chaperone. What a to-do that caused!"

"I take it you harbour no such intentions."

"Goodness, no! You're quite safe there, Mrs Peel. Besides, Mr Peel wouldn't take too kindly to it, would he?"

Augusta chose not to reply.

Gabriel filled the silence. "It's just my luck that the girl I'm really keen on should be accompanied by a chaperone. I can't help it, though. When I think back to the moment I first saw her – accompanying those pupils of hers on a trip to see *St George and the Dragon* – I remember seeing all those grubby children and then this… this *vision* of a girl. That's the only way I can describe her. Radiant, she was; just sheer beauty. The moment she appeared in my theatre I convinced myself that I'd died and gone to heaven! Really, I did." His head nodded in contemplation. "So I shall be *extremely* kind to her, Mrs Peel. Just you wait and see."

"I'm pleased to hear it."

"I want you to give good reports of me to Mrs Jones. Is she a close friend of yours?"

"Fairly close."

"You don't give much away, do you?"

"It depends on the company I'm keeping. This evening I'm merely serving as a chaperone. You don't really need to speak to me at all."

"Ah, but I like speaking to you! People interest me, you see. I've always been fascinated by human nature. What are your hopes and dreams, Mrs Peel?"

Augusta laughed to cover her growing sense of unease. "Now is not the time to discuss such things."

"Sum them up for me, then. Just a few words. What do you want from life?"

"I've already had all I want from life."

"Really?" He leaned in toward her. "I don't believe you, Mrs Peel. You must want something. *Everyone* wants something."

"All I want is a quiet life."

He glanced over his shoulder. "Oh, look. Harri's coming back."

Augusta followed his gaze to see a glimmer of blue sweeping across the restaurant.

"There's one thing I've learned about people, Mrs Peel," he said as they watched Harriet approach. "Those who say they want a quiet life rarely mean it."

Chapter 3

"Do you think he liked me?" Jean Taylor asked Cissy Drummond.

They stood shivering in a pool of light beneath a lamp post on Charing Cross Road, attempting to hail a taxi cab. The street's many shops had closed for the evening, but lights glimmered in the windows of numerous restaurants and public houses.

A taxi slowed to a halt and Cissy lowered her hand. "Gerrard Street," she said to the driver. "Flo's Club."

He opened the door and the two ladies climbed in.

Cissy flicked her pocket mirror open as soon she was seated. "Oh, it's too dark to see a thing! I should have done it while we were standing in the light."

"Did you hear my question?" persisted Jean. "Do you think he'll take me on?"

"It's difficult to say." Cissy attempted to apply her lipstick in the dark, the task becoming even trickier as the taxi turned a corner. "Oh, forget it. A fine state I'm going to look when we get there!"

"He's been your agent for ten years, Cissy. Surely you know him well enough to tell."

Cissy sighed. Jean was starting to irritate her. She would do her best to lose her once they were inside the club. "Maurice Shepherd plays his cards close to his chest," she responded. "Always has done. He'll telephone once he's made up his mind."

"I don't have a telephone."

"He'll telephone *me*. That's what we agreed, wasn't it?" Cissy doubted she would hear from him any time soon, but she telling her friend that would put her in a terrible mood.

"I hope he likes me. I haven't worked for three months! It's taken a long time to recover from *The Parlour Game*."

"That wasn't your fault."

"Not *solely* mine, but I was on stage when the audience booed us off. And on the opening night as well! I'll never live it down. Perhaps my career's already over."

"Nonsense." Cissy sounded confident, but she had long shared a similar worry. An actress's career could be short, as there was always someone younger and prettier waiting in the wings. She had been trying to console herself with the thought of her impending marriage to American banker Grant Reynolds. She hardly knew the man, but he had tonnes of money and lived in Los Angeles. A career in Hollywood had to be on the cards for her.

"It isn't nonsense," lamented Jean. "Everything came to a horrible end three months ago. I lost my job and my husband all in one go."

"You weren't married."

"We were *almost* married!"

Cissy could just make out Jean's doll-like features in the gloom. Without a doubt she was the prettier of the two. Her large eyes and rosebud cheeks had made her a popular chorus girl back in the day. Twelve years later, however, it was talent that mattered, and Jean didn't have a great deal of that.

"That's men for you," said Cissy. "They go around proposing marriage, then callously change their minds."

"We met up a few days ago."

"Why?"

"Because I'm still in love with him!"

Cissy shook her head and offered Jean a cigarette. "You need him to regret ending the engagement. How are you to achieve that if you're constantly at his beck and call?"

"It's so difficult when you love someone."

Cissy groaned and lit up. "They're not worth it, Jean. Really they aren't."

"I'd probably think about him less if I had a proper job to distract me. It's all right for you."

"Why's it all right for me?"

"Because you're successful!"

"I don't know about that."

"Oh, you know you are. You've been given the starring role in *The Girl from Bentalls*, one of London's most popular plays! You've already been in moving pictures, and I'm sure you'll be in many more, especially when you move to America. Would you believe I was turned down for the role of a slave girl last week? They wouldn't even take me on as a *slave*!"

"The *role* of a slave girl, not an *actual* slave. There's a big difference." Cissy turned toward the window and looked out at the lights of Soho.

"Well, you must do whatever you can to persuade Mr Shepherd. I'm going half-mad about it."

"So am I."

"I've another audition tomorrow, but I'm not holding out much hope."

Cissy's teeth clenched. "You'd have a lot more success

if you didn't feel so dreadfully sorry for yourself all the time, Jean."

"What did you say?"

"You heard what I said."

The taxi came to an abrupt halt and the driver opened the door. Cissy stepped out and paid the fare with Jean following behind, a scowl on her face.

"Is that Cissy Drummond?" came a voice from the darkness.

Someone gave an impressed whistle and a young couple scurried up to her.

"It *is* you!" The man grinned. "Cissy Drummond! I saw you last year in *The American Widow*. You were wonderful!"

"Thank you. That's so kind of you." She rearranged her fur stole and flashed him her best smile.

His companion couldn't take her eyes off Cissy's outfit. "Your dress is beautiful! How many beads does it have sewn onto it?"

"I've no idea. Several thousand, I would say."

They laughed.

"I hope you don't mind me asking, but could you please sign your autograph on this?" The woman handed her a little notebook and pencil. "It's just something I use for my shopping lists. I never imagined Cissy Drummond might actually write on it!"

"Of course." Cissy scrawled her looping signature on the blank page and handed it back. "Now, you must excuse me. I'm on my way to meet some friends and I'm running late."

Jean stayed glued to Cissy's side as she made her way to the entrance of Flo's Club. "That must have been nice. But then I suppose you're used to it."

"It only ever happens when I'm dressed up."

"I wonder if people would be quite so nice to you if they knew the things I know."

"Such as?"

"Oh, you know." Jean gave a casual shrug. "The sort of things you prefer to keep quiet."

The club's proprietress, Florence Morrell, was seated in the reception box just inside the open door. Her dark skin glistened in the subdued light as she wafted a large feather fan beneath her face. Beside her stood a broad-shouldered doorman wearing a white dinner jacket and bow tie. He and Cissy exchanged a smile as she paid the admission fee.

"I have a message for you from Mr White, Mr Costello," she said to him. "Will you be in the lounge later?"

"Absolutely, Miss Drummond." He gave a reverent bow.

Cissy swept past him, her mind returning to the comment Jean had made moments earlier.

Had she meant it as a veiled threat?

Chapter 4

MISS DRUMMOND HAS some nerve suggesting we meet inside the club, thought Laurence Costello. *Surely there'll be witnesses.* He shifted from one foot to the other and nodded a greeting to two gentlemen in cheap suits as they walked toward him. Each handed over the entrance fee and went on their way.

"Looks like Blue Branch are in again tonight, Mrs Morrell," Laurence said.

"They seem to be in most nights," replied Florence.

"Not bad work if you can get it, eh? Spying on night-clubs to see if they're serving drinks after licensing hours."

"And enjoying a drink or two with me paying them just as handsomely as their employer." She gave him a wink. "Blue Branch won't give us any trouble, at least. I'm more worried about some of the others I've seen coming in this evening. I haven't refused anyone entry yet, because doing so is often more trouble than it's worth. You'll keep an eye on them, though, won't you?"

"Will do, madam." He puffed out his chest and assumed the air of a man in charge.

A naval officer paid for himself and his glamorous

companion. Once they were out the way, five drunken students dressed in tweed tried to barter over the entrance fee.

"I'll agree to forty shillings for the five of you," said Florence, "but nothing less. And you'd better behave yourselves. I've thrown men twice your size out of here."

Laurence cracked his knuckles as the students timidly darted past. Those sorts of chaps rarely caused problems, but they could become a touch troublesome if they drank too much and annoyed a bad-tempered gangster. They hurried toward the staircase that led down to the dance floor in the club's basement.

A shiny Daimler pulled up outside.

"Here's the Arabian prince I was telling you about, Laurence. I think he's decided he likes the place. Aren't we lucky?"

The dark-skinned man wore a suit that looked as if it had come straight off the Savile Row rack. He was accompanied by four attendants.

"Nothing to pay tonight!" Florence called out in the voice she reserved for clients with a questionable grasp of the English language. "Just go on in!"

She waved the group through and Laurence gave them a gracious bow. Royalty and Hollywood actors were the most revered guests at Flo's Club. They always spent plenty of money and drew a good crowd.

"That's almost three hundred in now, madam," he said, consulting the tally counter in his hand.

"Wonderful. I do like the busy nights, don't you? While I think of it, I'm going to see a new building tomorrow that's just become available in Wardour Street."

"A second club, madam?"

"Exactly. This place is getting busier each month, and I'm confident we'll be able to fill the new one just as easily.

It'll cost quite a bit to fit out, and the finances will be tight at the beginning, but it'll soon pay its way. I was wondering if you'd like to run it."

"Me?"

"Yes, you, Laurence. Why do you look so surprised? You've worked for me for a good few years now. You work hard and you've a solid understanding of how these places are run. I'll be there as well, of course, but I'd like to divide my time between the two venues, so I'll need someone reliable to run it. You're one of the few people I trust. What do you say?"

"I'd be very honoured to. Thank you, madam." Laurence knew he wasn't capable of it, but how could he say no? It was impossible. She completely relied on him and had just said he was one of the few people she trusted. He tried to ease a sharp pang of guilt by taking a deep breath.

"Are you all right, Laurence?"

"Absolutely fine, madam. A little surprised, but very honoured. Thank you for asking me."

"Good. Well, we can talk more about it tomorrow. I'm seeing the place at twelve. Oh, here comes Billy Kemery. Keep a close eye on him this evening, won't you? Any trouble, call for me directly."

"I will. I think it's safe to say that he's rather scared of you, madam. Everyone's a little scared of you, in fact."

"What nonsense, Laurence. I'm a pussy cat; you know that. Although I do have good reason for keeping a man of your size by my side."

He bit his lip and nodded. It looked set to be a busy evening. There were a few troublemakers to keep an eye on, including Billy Kemery, and a request from Cissy Drummond. Laurence's mind was already beginning to race.

Chapter 5

"JUST HALF AN HOUR! Surely you can't argue with that, Mrs Peel? Half an hour and then I'll let you take Harri back to Mrs Jones."

Augusta had eventually relented and let Gabriel Lennox drive her and Harriet from the restaurant to Flo's Club. The distance between the two was only a hundred yards, but the short journey had enabled him to show off in his motor car with the roof folded down.

Harriet and Gabriel sat sipping champagne at a table by the dance floor, occasionally shouting into each other's ears. Normal conversation was impossible over the noise of the jazz band. Balloons and streamers mingled with the crowd of energetic dancers. A woman in gold sequins lay sprawled on the floor, laughing hysterically as her partner attempted to haul her back to her feet.

Augusta sipped her brandy and tapped her foot to the music. This was as close as she ever came to dancing these days. If she'd known they would be ending up somewhere glamorous, she would have worn something a little less dowdy than a plain blouse and skirt. At least her auburn hair had been recently waved, and she had visited the cloakroom to apply more rouge and lipstick. There was no doubt, however, that she looked like a middle-aged chaperone, frequently glancing at her charge and anxiously checking her watch.

It was half-past eleven. Harriet was supposed to be home by now. Dorothy would be pacing the floor, and there would no doubt be a telling-off in store when Augusta finally got her there.

She drained her drink and wondered if she should order another. It was illegal to sell alcohol after ten, but most nightclubs did so regardless. Laws that had been brought in during the war were still in place three years later, which made little sense given that the times had changed so much.

She made her way through the throng to find a waiter, the smell of tobacco mingling with perfume and the floor sticky with slops of drink. Searching for a white jacket, she caught sight of a familiar face instead.

No, it can't be him. Not the man in the trench coat who was standing outside the draper's shop.

She spun on her heel and walked in the opposite direction. The crowd whooped in response to a saxophone solo and a shower of confetti rained down on the revellers. The drums were beating faster and faster, as if echoing the thud of her heart.

Did he follow me here?

"Fancy a drink?" asked a rowdy soldier, slapping his hand down on her shoulder.

Augusta shrugged him off and kept moving. She felt the need to get out of the club's basement and up to ground level. Perhaps she could persuade Harriet to leave. It wouldn't be easy, as she seemed extremely taken with Mr Lennox. How Augusta longed to go home. *But what if he stands outside my flat again?* Her mind lurched from one panicked thought to another.

Disorientated, she realised she was standing at the opposite side of the room from the staircase she had been heading toward, hoping to hide herself away in a quiet corner of the ground-floor lounge. She calmed herself with a deep breath, then started making her way back across the basement.

He stepped in front of her, blocking her path.

She recoiled, expecting a confrontation. Four years had passed since they had last met. Thoughts of that terrible day still haunted her.

He wore a dark lounge suit and his face was long and lean. His sharp grey eyes held hers, unblinking. He leaned forward and spoke in her ear in a strong French accent. "I must talk with you."

Perhaps I can pretend I don't remember him.

"Who *are* you?" she shouted back.

"Liège," he said with a frown. "You don't remember?"

"I've never been there."

She tried to step past him, but he took her arm.

"Please don't pretend, Mrs Peel."

"I've no idea what you're talking about, and if you don't let go of my arm I'll call one of the doormen over to help me."

Glancing around, she caught sight of the soldier who had offered to buy her a drink. She waved at him and smiled as she successfully attracted his attention.

As he stepped toward her, the Frenchman's grip on her arm loosened.

"I have to go," she said, pulling herself free. Looping arms with the soldier, she moved quickly away.

Chapter 6

CISSY DRUMMOND ANNOUNCED that she needed to powder her nose.

"I'll come with you!" responded Jean, picking her handbag up from the table.

Cissy had hoped for a momentary break from her friend, but it clearly wasn't to be. She pushed the earlier animosity from her mind and enjoyed a slow promenade toward the ladies' cloakroom. Heads turned in her direction and faces smiled as she moved. She responded with an expression she had perfected when greeting her delighted public: enigmatic and alluring. The golden rule was to always walk slowly. People needed time to stare.

The ladies in the cloakroom maintained a respectful distance as Cissy touched up her make-up in the floor-to-ceiling mirror.

Jean flung herself into a velvet easy chair. "Oh, this is comfy! I think we should spend the rest of the evening here. At least we'd be able to hear our conversation that way."

"Never take a seat within twenty yards of a lavatory,

Jean. Has no one ever taught you such things?" She patted a drooping curl back into shape as a chuckle from her captive audience reverberated around the room.

"Why's there a chair here, then?"

"It's there for people who are feeling tired and emotional. A state I thoroughly intend to be in myself before the evening's out."

More laughter followed.

"Then you might end up sitting in this chair after all," responded Jean.

Cissy allowed the ensuing silence to hang in the air. *Poor Jean. No one ever finds her amusing, no matter how hard she tries. What if I become like Jean one day?* Cissy's eyes hollowed in the mirror as she entertained the thought for a brief moment. *All it takes is one failed show, one failed performance... a scandal, even. What was it Jean said when we walked into the club earlier? Something about whether people would be so nice to me if they knew what I was keeping quiet.*

What does Jean know about me, anyway? Quite a bit, as it happens.

That was why Cissy had agreed to introduce Jean to her agent. Nothing would ever come of it, of course, but she had to at least pretend to help her old colleague out.

Poor Jean. The phrase kept echoing in her mind. Cissy genuinely felt sorry for her friend sometimes. She couldn't imagine what it would be like to have one's heart set on a career that could never come to anything. *Was it down to talent or luck?*

Cissy liked to think it was talent, but there had to be an element of luck involved as well. And then there was good luck and bad luck, and the space between the two was narrow.

Cissy dropped her lipstick into her bag and reassured herself that marrying Grant Reynolds was her ticket to

EMILY ORGAN

success. *If a Hollywood studio dithers about hiring me, Grant's money might just persuade them.*

A lady approached and congratulated Cissy on her recent performance in *The Girl from Bentalls*.

Cissy gushed her gratitude and explained that the play's success had all been down to her wonderful director and thoroughly professional co-stars. She added that the script was also the best she had ever come across.

As she spoke, she felt Jean's sullen eyes resting on her. *How will Jean respond when she finds out that Mr Shepherd isn't the least bit interested?*

There's no time to dwell on that now.

Cissy was beginning to feel a little weary.

It was time to find Laurence Costello.

Chapter 7

"AND THE NEXT time I saw him after that, he had mashed potato all over his face!"

The soldier had a lot of stories to tell. His tales were making the conversation a little one-sided, but Augusta didn't mind that.

She wiped a hand over the ear he had been shouting into for the past fifteen minutes and decided to make her excuses. "I have to find my charge and get her home."

"What?"

"I have to leave. Thank you for the drink."

There had been no sign of the man from Liège for a while. She could only hope that he had left the club.

"Must you go?" The soldier pushed out his bottom lip and sulked like an overgrown schoolboy.

A shrill whistle cut through the music. All of a sudden, light flooded the room and cries rang out from across the crowd. People pushed past her, glasses smashed.

What's happening?

Men in blue uniforms stampeded down the staircase from the ground floor.

"Police!" called an authoritative voice. "Everyone line up against the wall!"

There was no more music; just shouting, thudding and crashing.

Augusta lost sight of the sulking soldier and moved with the crowd, drifting past scattered chairs and an upended table. The floor was slippery with drink.

It's a raid, she realised. *The club was serving alcohol outside licensing hours and we've all been caught out.*

"Is there a way out?" muttered a man as he pushed past her. "There has to be a way out!"

Augusta bumped into a girl whose face was streaked with dark mascara.

"We're all going to be arrested!" the girl sobbed.

Augusta reluctantly took her place against the wall alongside dancers, military men, students and aristocrats. There were a few shifty-looking types among the club's clientele, but everyone had been there enjoying themselves and Augusta felt a pang of indignation that their fun had been ruined.

Where's Harriet? Dorothy will be livid about this. There can't be many young women who've been arrested under the supervision of a chaperone.

With great relief, Augusta caught sight of her charge, distinctive in her blue dress, over on the far side of the room. Harriet was crying and Gabriel had his arm around her.

The police officers were questioning people in turn and writing the information down in their notebooks. Regardless of occupation and status, they would all be summoned to the courthouse in the morning and ordered to pay a fine.

Augusta cast an anxious glance at Harriet. The poor girl had never experienced anything like this before. There just might be a way out, however. Augusta had a trick up her sleeve.

But is it worth my while?

She patiently waited until her turn came.

"Name?" asked the bored constable, his pencil poised.

"Who's in charge here?"

"The sergeant."

"Sergeant who?"

He rolled his eyes. "Can you just tell me your name, madam?"

"I'd like to speak with the sergeant, please."

"There's no talking your way out of this; you've all been caught red-handed. Name please, madam. We don't want to be here all night."

"You're all from Vine Street, I suppose. I don't think I know any of the sergeants there at the moment, but I'm sure my good friend Detective Inspector Fisher would fill me in if I were to ask him."

The constable looked her up and down, apparently deducing that her sensible clothes seemed a little out of place. "How do you know DI Fisher?"

"I'm sure he'll tell you when you mention my name."

Chapter 8

"WHAT A HORRIBLE EVENING!" Harriet buried her face in her hands. "And poor Gabe!"

"It's *Gabe* now, is it?"

"That's what all his closest friends call him. How could we just leave him there, Mrs Peel?" Harriet dropped her hands and turned to face Augusta. "He'll be arrested!"

The taxi conveyed them along Shaftesbury Avenue. The streets were quiet now that the theatres had closed.

"I'm confident that Gabe can look after himself."

"But you managed to get me out of that mess. Why not him?"

"Because he can sort himself out. Besides, this probably isn't the first time he's been arrested."

"How can you say such a thing?"

"Oh, I'm sure he won't have been apprehended for anything worse than drinking at a nightclub outside licensing hours. He's a regular at Flo's Club, isn't he?"

"I think so."

"There you go, then. He can look after himself. Are you shaking, Harriet?"

The girl held her hands out. "I think so. A little. Oh, it was a terrible shock when the police came in like that, wasn't it? I wish we'd never gone to that place now. It was fun with all the dancing and what have you, but I didn't realise we'd get into trouble for it. Mother must never know where we've been. You won't tell her, will you?"

"It's going to be rather difficult to hide it. We're an hour and a half late!"

"Oh, she's going to be so cross!"

"Yes, she is."

"We'll have to lie!"

"She won't believe us if we say we were sitting in the restaurant until one o'clock. Let's tell her that you and Gabriel wanted to have a dance at a club and then we lost track of time. And let's not mention anything about consuming alcohol after ten."

"She won't like it. She'll never let me go out with him again!"

"With all due respect to your mother, Harriet, you're nineteen now, and in theory you can make your own choices about such things. Don't tell her I said that, though."

"She gets so awfully cross with me. I can't bear it."

Augusta reached out and patted her charge's hand. With a bit of luck, Dorothy would never ask her to chaperone Harriet again. "I'll take responsibility for our misdemeanour this evening."

"Thank you, Mrs Peel."

"It was my duty to look after you, although I can't say it's altogether easy with a character like Gabriel Lennox around."

"He's quite delightful, isn't he?"

"That's one way of describing him."

"You don't agree?"

"I'm sure my opinion on the subject matters very little to you, Harriet. But I'll say this, for what it's worth. Men like Gabriel Lennox often find themselves in sticky situations and are liable to drag others down with them. I'll take responsibility for what happened this evening, but I may not be able to cover for him if there's ever a next time."

"I still don't understand how you got us out of there. Do you know someone in the police service?"

"Sort of."

"But how? You're not a policewoman, are you? Were you ever a policewoman?"

"No."

"So what then?"

"I just happened to mention an old friend of mine."

"I don't recall you telling me about a policeman friend before."

"I don't tell you everything about myself, Harriet."

"Well, I think you should. I might discover something interesting."

"I doubt it. I'm a middle-aged lady who enjoys repairing books."

"Oh, poor Gabe!" The girl's mind had clearly switched back to the police raid. "His poor little face when I left him standing there! I shall telephone him tomorrow. I hope he won't be angry with me for leaving him there like that!"

Chapter 9

GABRIEL LENNOX LEANED back against his car and lit a cigarette. All was quiet. The last of the police officers strode down the street toward Vine Street station, their notebooks filled with names and addresses. He would see all the partygoers again in the morning, their faces pale and tired. Onlookers would no doubt gather outside the police court to catch a glimpse of the club's famous and glamorous clientele.

It was very sneaky of Harri to get away like that. And with Mrs Peel talking round a policeman! How did she manage that?

He climbed into his car, started it up and drove off, enjoying the rush of air against his face. Although it was grimy London air, it felt refreshing after the pandemonium of the hot, noisy club.

He caught sight of a friend peering into the window of a bookshop on Charing Cross Road and pulled up, tossing his cigarette into the road.

"Raffy!" he called out. "It's closed!"

His friend, a fellow member of the Garrick Club, staggered over to the car, hands in his pockets and hair flopping into his face.

"What's closed?" His speech was slurred.

"That shop you were looking into. Come on, I'll give you a lift home."

Raffy climbed in and Gabriel pulled away.

"Marylebone, isn't it?" he asked his passenger.

"What is?"

"Where you live."

"Oh, yes. Yes. Marylebone. Taunton Place. It's very nice there, actually. I like it." Raffy's head rolled around as though he had lost all the strength in his neck.

"Good. Were you in Flo's Club this evening?"

"No, that other place. Forget what it's called now. Where are we going?"

"I'm taking you home, Raffy."

"Thank you. How very kind of you. You always were a good sort of chap. How are you, Gabe?"

"If you'd asked me that two hours ago, I'd have said, 'I've never been happier.' Only it's turned out to be a bit of a strange evening."

"How so?"

"Police raid at Flo's. Ruined everyone's fun, it did. I was with the most marvellous girl, and now she's been dragged away by her chaperone. A good thing, as it turns out. I wouldn't have wanted her getting in any trouble."

Raffy laughed and his head fell back. "A chaperone? What sort of girl has a chaperone these days?"

"My thoughts exactly, although I'm quite relieved she has someone looking after her given tonight's turn of events. She needs looking after."

"All ladies need looking after."

Gabriel swung the car left into Oxford Street, enjoying

the empty roads. "Good at looking after the ladies, are you?"

"Yes. Very good at it. Yes."

"Well, this young lady's got to me, you see. If you can call her a lady, that is; she's still a girl, really. It's rather taken me by surprise, it has. I don't quite know what to do about it, in fact. And now I've got to make decisions. That's what I've got to do. I don't believe I've ever felt this way about a girl before, and yet… Oh, I don't know, Raffy. That's why I'm going for a drive. To clear my head."

"Good idea. Chaps like us always need a clear head."

"She's not an actress, you know. She's a sewing mistress."

"Who? Charlotte?"

"No, it was all over with Charlotte a long time ago, remember? I'm talking about Harriet. She's a sewing mistress, not an actress for once!" He noticed Raffy rummaging in his jacket pocket. "What are you looking for?"

"This." He pulled out an enormous cigar.

"Good Lord! Where'd you get that?"

"No idea." He attempted to light it.

"So, as I was saying, I met Harriet when she brought a bunch of ghastly children into my theatre, and that was that. Completely smitten, I was."

"That's nice. This won't light."

"That's because we're travelling in a car with the roof down. There's too much wind. Light it when you get back home; we're nearly there now. Now, where was I? Ah yes, back to Harriet. It's wonderful spending time with someone who's not in the theatre business. Sometimes you forget there's an entirely different world out there! Perhaps it would do me good to leave London altogether."

"Leave? Why would you want to leave?"

"Oh, I don't know. My eyes have been opened up to a new world. Perhaps I could persuade Harriet to leave, too. Only, I think it might be rather difficult to separate her from her mother. Where are we now? Ah, Baker Street. Almost there. You're practically Sherlock Holmes's neighbour, Raffy."

"He's not real, you know."

Gabriel returned home after dropping Raffy off, parking outside a block of flats on Glasshouse Street. As he trudged up the stairs, he suddenly felt sober. The euphoric part of the evening seemed like a distant memory. Once inside the flat, he headed straight for the bathroom, turned the taps on and began to wash his clothes.

Chapter 10

THE SHRILL of whistles echoed in Harriet's aching head. *All those police officers, and in such a confined space!* Her heart raced at the memory of it.

"Miss Jones, could you please thread my needle again?"

Harriet turned away from the window. "Of course, Angela."

She took the needle and thread from the girl's chubby fingers. She usually encouraged the girls to thread their own needles, but she had shown Angela enough times before and no longer had the patience.

"Thank you."

"How are you getting on with that patch?"

Angela held up the apron, which was a good deal grubbier than it had been twenty minutes earlier. "I started it, but I can't get it straight."

"I see what you mean." Harriet stared at the rapidly fraying patch and tried to think of something encouraging to say. "It might be best if you start again, Angela. But don't worry, I'll help you."

"I've finished mine," came a voice as a neatly patched apron was pushed under Harriet's nose.

"Well done, Susanna. Perhaps you could do another one."

"Another one?"

"Yes. See if you can make it even more perfect."

As Harriet unpicked Angela's sewing, her mother's scolding from the previous evening returned to her ears. She had never seen her mother so angry before. The noise she had made was worse than the police whistles. Dorothy had decreed that Harriet was never allowed to see Gabriel again.

I should never have let him take me to that place; it had been a foolish idea.

Harriet never wanted to set foot in a nightclub again, but she certainly wanted to see Gabriel. Despite the events of the previous evening, she cared about him more than she had ever cared about anyone, and she was sure he felt the same. She just needed to find a way to see him without her mother finding out.

A sewing mistress's salary wasn't generous, but perhaps it would be enough to secure some lodgings. Harriet conjectured that she would have more freedom if she moved out of her mother's house. She could lodge with a nice family or perhaps a pair of respectable spinsters. *Surely Mother couldn't object to that.* She wondered if Gabriel might know of a room somewhere. He knew so many people in London, though it was unlikely that he knew any respectable spinsters.

"Can you thread my needle, please, Miss Jones?" came another voice.

"Of course."

Harriet imagined the court hearing would be over by now. *How has Gabriel fared?* He wouldn't be happy about paying a fine. He'd told her he needed every penny he had to fund the production of *An Evening Swansong* he was working on.

He works so hard, yet he's so much fun, too. Funny and adorable. Harriet couldn't stop thinking about him.

"Ouch!" She lifted her finger to her mouth to soothe the pain.

"Are you all right, Miss?"

"Never get distracted while threading a needle, Laura."

"Did you get distracted?"

"Yes, I did. Silly me."

Harriet yawned, having barely slept the previous night. The clock on the classroom wall showed that it was just after one. *Only another half an hour of mending aprons.*

"I don't like sewing, Miss," said Angela sulkily.

Harriet smiled, feeling a deep empathy for the girl she often saw standing alone in the playground. "Come and sit by me and we'll do it together. You'll do very well at it in time. Just you wait and see."

Chapter 11

PERCHED ON HER STOOL, Augusta threaded a needle beneath her work light and started stitching together the final section of pages to the text block of Thomas J Shepperton's *Collected Poems*. The repair was progressing well. The cover had been cleaned and she had created a new spine. The green she had used didn't quite match the cover, but it was close enough. After the noise and chaos of the previous evening, Augusta was grateful for the calm of her workshop and the soothing rumble of trains beneath her feet.

A knock sounded at the window. It was Dorothy again.

Augusta sighed. *How can she have anything left to say?*

She pushed the needle beneath a stitch and felt her teeth clench. She understood why Dorothy had been so angry, and had already apologised profusely for her part in it. But if she were here to deliver another telling off, Augusta would have to resort to chasing her friend out of there. Her father's old carpenter's square would come in handy if so.

Dorothy bustled through the door, a shopping basket

looped over her arm. "I take it you've seen the papers today?" Her eyes were wide behind her spectacles.

"Not yet, no."

"Not yet? I suppose you've been down here all day. You'll have no idea what happened at Flo's Club last night, in that case."

"The raid?"

"That was mentioned, yes. But something much worse than that."

"What is it?"

"You really haven't heard, have you? There was a murder!"

"Really?!" Augusta put down her needle and sat back in her chair.

"Yes! An actress was shot dead. I forget her name now. I assumed you'd seen the papers like everyone else, so I didn't bother bringing mine with me."

"But how? I don't understand. Why didn't we hear about it at the time?"

Dorothy shrugged. "I don't know how anyone goes to a place where someone has been murdered and doesn't hear about it."

"How horrible. The poor woman. It must have happened after we left."

"I can only hope it did. It might have been Harriet lying there dead, otherwise! Can you imagine?"

"I wonder how it happened." Augusta thought about the shifty types she had seen at the club. Perhaps an altercation had broken out and the woman had been shot by mistake. "Did the papers say whether anyone has been arrested?"

"No one's been arrested yet."

"There must have been witnesses. There were hundreds of people there last night."

"She was found in one of the upstairs rooms."

"Then it could have happened without anyone realising."

"I suppose it must have done. How on earth you allowed my daughter to be taken there, I'll never know."

"I've already apologised for that, Dorothy."

"It's a nightclub, Augusta! Things like this always happen at nightclubs. All that music, dancing and alcohol. And the people you find in those places! They have a complete disregard for everything we've all been through over the past decade. Many are from the criminal classes, of course. Women of ill repute, sinister men selling drugs…" She shook her head. "I can't tell you how disappointed I was that you allowed my daughter to go there."

"I sensed the measure of your disappointment last night. Aren't you the least bit pleased that I managed to keep Harriet out of court today?"

"I suppose I should be grateful for that. She told me you knew one of the policemen."

"Yes."

"How?"

"Oh, just an old friend. You said you don't remember the actress's name, didn't you?"

"Yes, and it didn't mean anything to me when I read it. I suspect she was a bit of a nobody."

Chapter 12

"Come down from there, Sparky!" Augusta stood waiting with her hands on her hips. "It's time for bed."

The little yellow bird cocked his head, then flew from the curtain rail to the top of the bookcase.

"No, not there. Come on, into your cage. I've chopped up some apple for you. It's nice and fresh, but it'll start to go brown if you leave it any longer."

Lady Hereford had left strict instructions with regard to Sparky's routine. Between the hours of nine in the evening and seven in the morning he was to roost in his cage with a silk shawl draped over it. A routine was essential for a contented canary, according to Lady Hereford. In fact, a contented canary was more likely to sing. Augusta had known so little about canaries at the time that she had agreed to go along with it.

She had persuaded the bird to perch on her finger a few times on previous occasions. Perhaps she could do it again now. She retrieved a piece of apple from the cage, then stood beside the bookcase and held it up to him. He observed her closely as she raised her other hand and held out a finger as a small perch.

"Come along then, Sparky."

He didn't move.

Augusta fetched a footstool and climbed on to get a little closer to the bird. "Hop onto my finger and you can have this piece of apple."

After giving her another hard stare, he cautiously fluttered onto the makeshift perch. His little claws tickled slightly as they gripped her finger. As Sparky pecked at the apple, Augusta prepared herself to step off the stool and carry him over to his cage.

A sudden knock at the door startled her. The bird flew off over her head and she stepped back onto nothing. She cried out as she tumbled to the floor, knocking a lamp off the side table as she went.

The knock came again.

"All right!" she called out, picking herself up.

She limped over to the door, rubbing her elbow. Callers at this hour were unusual. "Who is it?"

"The police."

Her stomach clenched. They were obviously summoning her to appear in court; she hadn't got away with it after all. They would be after Harriet too, and then Dorothy would be even crosser with her. It was safe to say that she had lost a friend there. Not a close friend, fortunately.

She peered through the peephole in her door and saw a man in plain clothes.

A detective.

And not just any old detective. It was someone she knew.

He's probably here to give me a big telling off. He obviously wasn't prepared to leave it up to a constable.

Augusta unbolted the door and opened it.

The detective wore a rain-splashed trench coat over a dark suit and was leaning on a walking stick. His face broke out into a surprised smile of recognition. "So you're the mysterious Mrs Peel!"

"Mr Fisher!"

She hadn't seen him since the war. His eyes were narrow, with deeper crow's feet than before. His square jaw seemed a little softer and his hair was turning grey. He was also a little fatter than she remembered, though he probably would have said the same of her.

"Or should I call you Detective Inspector Fisher of Scotland Yard? You'd better come in."

He removed his hat and followed her into the living room. She smoothed her hair and wished she'd changed out of the scruffy pullover and slacks she had been wearing in her workshop all day.

"Please excuse my appearance."

"What's wrong with it?" A smile played on his lips.

"Work clothes. I wasn't expecting a visitor."

"You're forgetting that I've seen you in a number of strange guises before now."

"I suppose you have." She gestured for him to take a seat. "And I suppose you're here to discuss the events of last night. I apologise for using your name. It was rather cheeky of me, especially after all this time."

"I wasn't sure who the Mrs Peel they mentioned was, and that's why I came to see you. I knew you by a different name back then, of course."

"Indeed. I think I must have panicked when I asked for you. I was supposed to be chaperoning a girl but I wasn't doing a particularly good job of it. Delivering her home late was bad enough, but if she'd had to go to court today—"

"I understand." Detective Inspector Fisher sat and surveyed the room. "So this is where you live now. I wondered whether you'd ever turn up again."

"Like a bad penny?"

"Now, I didn't say that." He laughed. "How are you keeping?"

"Well, thank you. And you?"

"Very well."

She glanced at his stick. "You're walking now, I see."

"You make me sound like a small child. Yes, I've been walking for a few years now."

"How wonderful. They said you'd never—"

"They said a lot of things that turned out to be utter nonsense. Anyway, it's nice to see you again, Mrs Peel."

"Likewise. I presume you're here to reprimand me and summon me to court." She picked up the lamp she had knocked over and tried to push out the dent in its shade.

"No. Although I should say that it would be within my rights to do so. What happened to that lamp?"

"I was trying to catch a canary when you called, and I knocked it over. Where's he gone now, I wonder? Oh look, he's back on the curtain rail again. Hopeless. He's refusing to go to bed."

He smiled. "He has a strict bedtime, does he?"

"Yes, apparently so. He belongs to Lady Hereford, and she told me he must go to bed on time because it helps him sing. I've never heard him sing, which suggests to me that I'm not doing a very good job of that either." She gave up on the dented lampshade. "Would you like some coffee?"

"Thank you."

"Would you mind trying to put Sparky to bed while I'm at it? He doesn't listen to a word I say."

. . .

By the time she returned to the living room with the coffee tray, Detective Inspector Fisher was leafing through Shepperton's *Collected Poems* and Sparky was safely stowed in his cage.

"Well done! How did you manage that?" She placed the tray on the table and covered the cage with the silk shawl.

"He practically did it himself. He flew onto the back of that chair, so I wafted this book in his general direction and in he went. I've just read a rather nice poem about a singing shepherdess. Is this book a favourite of yours?"

"No. I was just repairing it."

"Were you indeed?" He examined its cover. "You're a woman of many talents, Mrs Peel. Come to think of it, wasn't your father a bookbinder?"

"Yes."

"I thought so." He cleared his throat. "I've an old favourite book that's fallen apart. I'd love to be able to read it again without it disintegrating completely. I could buy a new copy, I suppose, but I'm rather attached to the old one."

"I know the feeling."

"I'd pay you, of course. Don't feel you'd have to do it as a favour."

"Just bring it to my workshop whenever you're ready. It's down in the basement."

"I will do." He smiled. "Are you on the telephone here?"

"No, and I'm not in any rush to get one."

"I see." He straightened his tie, as if giving some thought to what he was about to say. "I don't know if you've heard, but there was a murder at Flo's Club last night. The Yard has been called in to assist C Division with the investigation."

"I read about it in the paper. I had no idea it had happened until a friend mentioned it to me."

"A young actress, Miss Jean Taylor, was found dead from a gunshot wound in a storage room. You probably gleaned that much from the newspaper reports."

"Yes. I read that she had been found by a member of staff during the early hours of this morning."

"She was indeed. The room isn't strictly open to guests, but it was just about accessible, and it wasn't unusual for people to use the place for a private chat, apparently."

"What time was she murdered?"

"Around midnight, we believe."

"That's when the raid occurred."

"Yes, it was at pretty much the same time."

"Surely someone must have heard the gun go off."

"You'd think so, wouldn't you? But there was a lot of noise at that time."

"I can vouch for that. And I suppose with all the commotion going on, no one realised what had happened."

"That's right. Her body wasn't discovered until half-past one. The assistant manager found her and raised the alarm."

"Was Florence Morrell still on the premises at that point?"

"No, she'd left by then. Only Mr Costello was present. He was doing a final check of the building before locking everything up."

"There were a few hundred people there. It'll be quite difficult for you to whittle down the suspects."

"It certainly will be, but we've learned a bit about Miss Taylor and already have a few people we're interested in talking to."

"Well, that sounds promising, I wish you luck with it. I

presume you'd like to know if I noticed anything suspicious. I didn't hear or see anything out of the ordinary, I'm afraid. And I've no idea who Miss Taylor was or what she looked like. The newspaper listed some of the plays she'd been in, but I haven't seen any of them. Do you have a photograph of her?"

"Just this one here."

He reached into his inside pocket and took out a picture of a woman with wide-set, long-lashed eyes, rosebud lips and shiny, waved hair.

"She's very pretty."

"This is a publicity photograph from about five years ago. Her hair was a little longer back then."

"I don't recognise her, I'm afraid."

"Not to worry." He popped the picture back in his pocket.

"And I didn't venture anywhere near the storage room, either. In fact, I don't remember seeing anything that struck me as suspicious. I may have seen something relevant without realising, I suppose."

He leaned forward and picked up his coffee. "I was wondering whether you might be willing to be a little more than a witness."

"What do you mean?"

"We could do with some help."

"Scotland Yard needs help? I doubt that very much. You've some of the best detectives in the country."

"Some of whom are busy working on a tricky case in the West Country. One of our superintendents is down there as well, as a matter of fact."

"I'm afraid I'm too busy."

"Repairing books?"

"There are so many books that need repairing. I'm quite happy to give you my own account of last night's proceedings if that's any use at all, but I really can't do any more than that."

"Aren't you the least bit interested in helping us?"

"I don't see how I can."

"I know what you're capable of, Mrs Peel."

She stared down into her coffee cup. *It had been a mistake to mention his name at Flo's Club. If only I'd kept quiet.* "Those times are behind me now. I don't want to be involved."

"That's a great shame," he said, taking a large gulp from his cup, "especially considering what you managed to achieve on that case in Bruges."

"I like to live a much simpler life these days."

"So I gather." An awkward pause followed. "Right, then." He picked up his walking stick and got to his feet. "Well, I apologise for interrupting your evening, Mrs Peel. It was a pleasure to meet Sparky."

Augusta stood as he limped over to the door.

"I saw Jacques last night," she ventured.

He stopped, one hand on the latch. "You spoke to him?"

"He tried to talk, but I managed to get away."

"Interesting."

"You've not seen him since—"

"No, I haven't seen him at all."

"I think I saw him in the street the other day as well. Just outside the window. He must know where I live."

"Perhaps you could let me know if he approaches you again."

"I will do."

"And perhaps I can persuade you to have another think about helping us out with the Jean Taylor case."

"I told you I—"

"Gabriel Lennox…"

Her stomach gave a flip. "What of him?"

"You know the man, don't you?"

"A little."

"He was engaged to Miss Taylor until recently, but he suddenly broke it off."

"Really?"

"As I say, Mrs Peel. Have another think." He opened the door, placed his hat on his head and walked out.

Chapter 13

HARRIET STEPPED out of the brick school building on Old Gloucester Street and put up her umbrella. She even managed to look graceful in a dull brown overcoat.

"Miss Jones!" A small girl ran up and handed her something.

Augusta couldn't quite see what it was from where she was standing.

Harriet smiled as the girl ran back to her mother, then continued walking over to where Augusta stood waiting on the corner of Queen Square.

"Mrs Peel! This is a surprise." She gave a pretty smile and the damp breeze whipped at her bobbed hair.

"A gift?" Augusta glanced down at the posy of damp autumn leaves in Harriet's hand.

"Yes, from little Angela. I don't suppose she could find any flowers to pick at this time of year. It was very thoughtful of her."

"I came here to speak to you about Flo's Club. You've heard what happened there, have you?"

"Yes! Dreadful, isn't it? Mother and I read about it in the paper."

"Have the police spoken to you?"

"No. Do you think they will?" She bit her lip.

"I imagine they'll want to speak to everyone who was at the club that evening, but I don't know that for certain."

"Do you think we'll be in trouble for not paying the fine?"

"I don't think so. They've more important matters to attend to now."

"Have the police spoken to you?"

"My friend from the Yard visited yesterday."

"And what did he say about it all?"

"He was interested to know whether I'd seen anything suspicious that evening."

"And had you?"

"No. Did you?"

"No, nothing at all. I suppose they'll come and ask me about it at some point." She drew in a deep breath. "I didn't like the way the police came charging in like that. It was quite frightening."

"Did you recognise the girl who was murdered?"

"No. I read that she was an actress, but I'd never heard of her before."

So Gabriel hasn't mentioned his former fiancée. No great surprise there.

"It's just awful," continued Harriet. "Who could do such a thing? I suppose there'll be a lot of officers working on a case like this."

"There will indeed. My friend told me Scotland Yard will also be involved. I hope they catch the culprit quickly. Have you spoken to Mr Lennox since that evening?"

"No. He sent me a telegram yesterday morning to check that I'd got home all right. I tried telephoning him yesterday evening, but there was no answer. I wonder if he knew her."

"I wonder if he did."

"We're lucky we got away before all that terrible business occurred."

"It may have happened while we were there. The police seem to think the murder occurred just as the raid began."

"Really? But surely we'd have known if someone had been shot."

"It was in an upstairs room, and with all the commotion going on downstairs I doubt many people would have heard it."

"So we were still there at the time? Oh, that really is terrible. The poor girl! I never want to go back to that horrible place again. I wish Gabe hadn't take us there, don't you?"

"I wish I'd persuaded him not to. I was far too pliant."

Harriet smiled. "But that's what makes you such a good chaperone."

"Not as far as your mother's concerned."

"It's a shame you won't be able to do it again. She'll probably insist on that awful Mrs Jenkins accompanying us next time we go out."

"You plan to go out with Mr Lennox again, do you? I thought your mother had forbidden it."

"I'll talk her round. I'll be unbearable until she agrees to it. I'll promise never to visit a nightclub with him again, but other than that I can't wait to see him. He's wonderful fun."

Judging by her enthusiastic expression, Harriet was completely oblivious of Gabriel's broken engagement with Jean Taylor.

"I wouldn't rush into anything."

"Why do you say that?"

"How much do you know about Mr Lennox?"

"We only met recently, but I know a good deal about him. He's quite forthcoming, and… well, I know he can be a little boastful at times, but it's all said in a spirit of good fun. Is there something particular I should know about him, Mrs Peel? I don't like the look on your face. You're beginning to worry me."

Augusta decided it wasn't her duty to tell her young charge what she knew. Gabriel would have to do that himself. "It wasn't my intention to worry you, Harriet, and I'm sorry if I did. Just be cautious, that's all, especially when you're dealing with a man who's a little older than you. He'll have a past, you know."

"What sort of past?"

"I don't know; I just thought I should mention it. I've met men like him before, you see."

"Have you, Mrs Peel? Do tell!"

"Another time. You just need to be careful."

Harriet pouted. "You're beginning to sound like my mother. I had a higher opinion of you, Mrs Peel."

Chapter 14

"MR LENNOX IS A VERY BUSY MAN," said the lady in the ticket office at the Olympus Theatre.

"I'm sure he is. Can you please tell him Mrs Peel is here to see him? Tell him it's about Harriet."

A short while later, Augusta found herself sitting in a leather chair in Gabriel's office. Photographs of him posing with various theatre stars hung on the red walls alongside a glass cabinet displaying several shiny awards. A pleasant scent of eau-de-cologne lingered in the air.

"It's always a delight to see you, Mrs Peel." He was in his shirtsleeves with a pale tweed waistcoat. He gave her a grin as he poured drinks from a decanter. "I enjoyed our little chat the other evening."

"The evening that ended in tragedy, you mean."

"Well, yes. An awful tragedy." He handed her a glass, leaned back against his desk and looked her up and down. "You're looking very smart today."

It was a feeble attempt to flatter her, but Augusta thanked him all the same.

"The blue of the jacket matches your eyes," he added.

"I recall you saying something similar to Harriet the other evening."

"Did I? Golly, that's rather embarrassing isn't it? I need to come up with some new conversation openers. How is Harri by the way?"

"She's all right. A little affected by the incident at the club, of course, but other than that she's quite well."

"That's a relief. I take full responsibility for dragging you both there, Mrs Peel. It was my idea, and I'm terribly sorry about it now. I must say that you did extremely well to escape the police round-up. And well done for getting Harri out of there when you did. She's far too young to be caught up in such nonsense, and lucky to have such a quick-thinking chaperone. You have your wits about you." He winked and sipped his drink. "I can only imagine you've come here with a message from Mrs Jones. Forbidden from seeing her daughter again, am I? It certainly wasn't my finest hour. If only I'd listened to you and we'd got her home straight after the restaurant."

"I don't have a message from Mrs Jones."

Gabriel raised an eyebrow. "What brings you here, then?"

"I'm keen to find out anything you might know about the murder that night."

"I don't know anything more than the next man, I'm afraid. Why do you ask?"

"You must have been particularly upset on hearing the news."

"It's extremely upsetting for everyone; not least the poor girl's family."

"But you knew her, didn't you? Jean Taylor."

"Ah." He took another swig from his glass, walked around the large desk and sat behind it. "As a matter of fact, I did."

"Did you see her that evening?"

"Only briefly, to say hello. I'm not sure how you know about that."

"Word spreads very quickly."

"Clearly."

"Have you told Harriet about her?"

"No." Gabriel ran a hand through his red hair. "I haven't spoken to Harri since that evening. I sent her a telegram the following day, but I was planning to telephone her in a day or two to find out whether her mother will permit me to see her again."

"Do you plan to tell her about your recent engagement to Jean Taylor?"

He gave an uneasy laugh. "You do know it was called off, don't you? And I'd like to know where you're getting all this information from. Just general gossip, is it?"

"If I was able to find it out easily enough, it won't be long before Harriet does."

"Well, it's no great secret. I just haven't got round to telling her about it yet. We're in the early stages of our courtship, and it wouldn't do for a chap to go spouting off about his previous love affairs right from the get-go, would it? I'm not a young fellow in the earliest bloom of youth; I'm thirty-one years of age. And although I've never discussed my past amours with Harri, I'm quite certain she isn't foolish enough to believe there haven't been any! I wasn't being dishonest or disingenuous, if that's what you're suggesting."

"I wasn't suggesting anything of the kind."

"Good! That's a relief."

"Hearing of Miss Taylor's death must have been very upsetting. I offer you my condolences."

"Thank you, Mrs Peel. It is extremely upsetting."

"How long did your engagement last?"

"About six months. I put an end to it, though I felt terribly bad for doing so. She was a delightful girl, but I realised I had no desire to marry her. I was planning to explain all this to Harri someday." He got to his feet and walked over to the window. "Now I'll have to explain it to her when we next meet. If I'm allowed to see her again, that is. If Mrs Jones forbids it, I suppose I shan't ever have a chance to explain myself."

"She's bound to find out about your relationship soon, and I think she should hear it from you."

He turned to face her. "Yes, I think that's probably a good idea, otherwise I shall be in the dog house before I know it. But what of your friends in the police?"

"It's just the one friend. What of him?"

"He sent you here, did he?"

"No. Why would he?"

"Because I used to be engaged to Jean Taylor. Your police friend might have asked you to elicit information from me. Not that I mind you doing so, Mrs Peel. I have nothing to hide and I can quite understand why they'd take an interest in me. There were hundreds of people at the club that night, and they'll need to narrow down their suspects by establishing some sort of link with her."

"I can assure you he hasn't sent me here. I simply came to suggest that you tell Harriet about your relationship with Jean Taylor before she finds out some other way."

"I see. Well, sorry about bringing up that stuff about the police. I'm a little anxious about the whole affair, as you can probably tell. I think your suggestion about being honest with Harri is an excellent one. Thank you for paying me this visit. I appreciate it." Gabriel reminded Augusta of a fox as he fixed her with his hazel eyes and smiled. "And thank you for not telling Harri about the engagement; it's extremely tactful of you. I'll do the right thing and explain it all to her in a letter. Do you think she'd appreciate a letter?"

"Yes, I think she would."

"Good. That settles it, then." He drained his glass and returned to his desk. "Poor Jean. I never imagined something like this would happen to her."

"How could you possibly have imagined it?"

"Indeed. It's quite out of the blue. And to top it all, I can already feel the finger pointing at me. Completely uncalled for. How anyone could even consider that I would do such a thing is beyond me!"

Chapter 15

A BRISK WIND blew in from the river and whipped around the imposing brick and granite buildings of New Scotland Yard.

Augusta paused at the gates. *Do I really want to do this?* She finally had the quiet life she had been seeking; time spent alone with books and the occasional favour for a friend. She was under no obligation to Detective Inspector Fisher. He would manage perfectly well if she refused to get involved. But Jean Taylor was another matter. *How can I just walk away from the murder of a young woman?*

It felt impossible.

She had effectively involved herself the moment she mentioned the senior officer's name at the nightclub. She would have to go through with it now.

Detective Inspector Fisher didn't seem surprised to see her, as if he had expected her to change her mind about the case and turn up in his office. The smell of tobacco lingered in the dingy, wood-panelled room.

"Any more approaches from our friend Jacques?" he asked after a young woman had deposited a tea tray on his desk.

"No. I'm hoping he's given up trying to talk to me by now."

"It was rather a surprise to discover that he's over here."

"He must want to confront me about Sarah."

The detective's eyes narrowed. "He shouldn't be allowed to; it's all water under the bridge now. I have no idea what he's playing at." His gaze rested on the teapot as he contemplated this thought. Then he put on a pair of spectacles and picked up his notebook. "Now then, the inquest into Miss Taylor's murder is to open tomorrow. Ten o'clock at Westminster Coroner's Court. Let's discuss Gabriel Lennox in the meantime."

"Have you spoken to him yet?"

"Not personally. One of the constables had a chat with him, which was all very pleasant but entirely unproductive, apparently. The men are working their way around everyone who knew Miss Taylor and happened to be in the club that evening. I'd be interested to hear your impression of Lennox."

"I don't know him well at all."

"But what's your impression of him?" He began to pour out the tea.

"He's charming, chatty and tells people what he thinks they want to hear. He talks about himself quite a bit, but that's to be expected of someone who works in the theatre business, I suppose."

"Do you think he might be hiding anything?"

"I'm sure he is."

"What makes you say that?"

"Just the look on his face. Though that's not always a reliable indicator, I know."

"A good enough one in my book. Sometimes you get a feeling about someone but can't quite put your finger on it."

"Exactly. When I spoke to him yesterday, he admitted he'd previously been engaged to Miss Taylor and that he hadn't told Harriet Jones about it yet. That was reasonably forthcoming of him, I would say."

"Harriet Jones is the young woman you were chaperoning that evening, isn't she?"

"That's right. I suggested he might need to tell her about the engagement."

"Why did you suggest that?"

"She's bound to find out about it soon enough, and probably from a newspaper if he doesn't. She'll be terribly upset about it."

"And would that be such a bad thing?"

"Yes. It would be much better if she heard it from him."

"You care about the girl's feelings, then?"

"I suppose I must do if I don't want to see her upset. I've only acted as her chaperone a few times, but I feel quite protective of her. She lost her father in the war, you see, and her mother... well, she's a friend of mine, but she's rather strict with poor Harriet. Perhaps I feel the need to be someone she can turn to if needs be. A bit like a spinster aunt, if that makes sense."

He smiled, then asked, "Were you worried about her spending time with Mr Lennox?"

"I was a little. And I still am, given that she still wants to see him. He's quite a bit older than her, and there's something rather innocent about Harriet. I don't want him taking advantage of her."

"An understandable worry. It'll be interesting to see her reaction to the news of his former engagement."

"I shouldn't think that was his first engagement, either. He strikes me as the sort of chap who'd have a few failed engagements behind him."

"Do you know that for certain or is it just a hunch?"

"Just a hunch."

"You'd say that he's a little impulsive, would you?"

"At a guess, I'd say so."

"And he doesn't seem to have a great deal of loyalty."

"Maybe not. Although he does seem very fond of Harriet."

"At the moment."

"Yes, at the moment. He must once have been very fond of Miss Taylor, too."

Chapter 16

AUGUSTA PUSHED her way through the throng outside Westminster Coroner's Court the following morning. Once inside, she squeezed onto the end of a bench in the crowded public gallery. There was clearly a lot of interest in this particular inquest.

Detective Inspector Fisher caught her eye from across the room and gave her a polite nod. The lively chatter around her fell silent as the coroner entered.

Jean Taylor's father was the first witness to speak. Quiet and forlorn, he leaned forward against the witness stand as he described his daughter's happy upbringing in Cambridgeshire. Augusta felt a lump in her throat as she heard him describe the childhood of a girl who had always wanted to be an actress, despite her father's best attempts to dissuade her. Her family had maintained little contact with her after she moved to London, and had last heard from her when she wrote to tell them of her engagement to Gabriel Lennox. He had heard nothing more from her after that.

The next witness, Maud Fletcher, had shared a flat

with Jean on Frith Street in Soho. Miss Fletcher, an aspiring actress who worked as a waitress, was tall with fair hair and an aquiline nose. She described her flatmate as friendly and ambitious, but said Jean had been plagued at times with anxiety about her career, which hadn't been as successful as she would have liked.

"I kept telling her she was more successful than me," said Miss Fletcher, "but it didn't stop her sinking into a state of melancholy now and again."

Miss Fletcher described how she had awoken on the morning of 6th October to find Jean's bedroom empty. She hadn't considered this unusual, as her friend occasionally stayed out all night. However, a police constable had visited her workplace later that day to tell her the sad news.

Augusta noticed a hushed ripple of excitement in the room when Cissy Drummond was called. The glamorous actress wore a fashionable black suit with a fur across her shoulders and a velvet cloche hat. There was something rather feline about her face, and her black-rimmed eyes flitted around the court as if to gauge her audience.

"Miss Cissy Drummond," said the coroner, "of Langham Place, Fitzrovia. Legally known as Edith Parkinson. Is that right?"

"That's right," she replied, her voice projecting perfectly.

"An actress who may be familiar to many in the court."

"Currently starring in *The Girl from Bentalls* at The Abacus. Tickets start at sixpence." She gave a whimsical smile.

"You were with Miss Taylor on the night of her death."

"That's correct."

"Perhaps you can tell us what you did that evening before visiting Flo's Club."

"It was all rather hurried. As soon as the show finished,

I changed out of my costume and we had a quick supper at Le Petit Chevalier on Charing Cross Road. It's one of my favourite places. The atmosphere is wonderful and the food is deliciously awful."

"Were you accompanied by anyone else?"

"My agent, Mr Maurice Shepherd, and my costumier, Mr Francis Masefield. It had been set up so that my agent and Jean could meet. She had been dropped by her own agent and was looking for a new one."

"Did Mr Shepherd agree to represent her?"

"It was just an initial meeting. The plan was for him to give it some thought and then telephone me about it. Jean was very keen on the idea, as she hadn't worked in three months. She was in *The Parlour Game*, you see. You heard what happened on opening night, I presume?"

The coroner shook his head.

"The entire cast was booed off. Hardly any of them have worked since, so we've started calling it 'The Parlour Curse'."

"Whose decision was it to visit Flo's Club?"

"Both mine and Jean's. We wanted to go on somewhere after dinner, but Maurice and Francis weren't fussed about joining us. Maurice doesn't like nightclubs and Francis wanted to head home to wash his hair."

This last comment raised a chuckle in the room, and Cissy's eyes gave an appreciative slow blink in response.

"How long had you known Miss Taylor?"

"We met twelve years ago while we were chorus girls in *All Aboard for Cairo!* It has an exclamation mark at the end. All the lines in that show had an exclamation mark at the end, in fact. It ran for thirteen weeks. Great fun, it was, but the jokes were prehistoric and our costumes were terribly twee."

"Your friendship was a close one, was it?"

"Not particularly, no. Bless her, Jean was the sort of friend who'd get in touch when things were going wrong. If you didn't hear a peep from her, you could only assume that all was well."

"So when you saw her that evening, things had been going badly?"

"Yes. Because of The Parlour Curse, as I've explained."

"And how was her mood that evening?"

"She was delightfully charming over dinner, then turned into a bit of a grouch afterwards. I think she was expecting Maurice to welcome her in with open arms. It never occurred to her that he might want a bit of time to think about it. But that's Maurice for you, and I tried explaining that to her. He never hurries over anything, you see. I once watched him spend ten minutes deciding which pen to sign a contract with."

"Did the change in her mood lead to a disagreement between you?"

"No, because we met with various other people as soon as we were inside the club."

"Who did you see her speaking to?"

"Oh, lots of people. I've given the police a list of names." She adjusted her fur and gave Detective Inspector Fisher a coy glance. "I can't recall them all now, but they've been written down in a little notebook somewhere. If you're wondering whether any of them struck me as the murdering type, I shall tell you now that they didn't. I didn't see anyone acting suspiciously, and Jean didn't tell me that anyone had been acting strangely toward her. Neither of us had any suspicion at all that such an awful thing was about to happen. Quite out of the blue, it was! It's just so terrible." She dabbed at the corner of each eye with a gloved finger.

"Were you aware that Miss Taylor had visited the storage room that evening?"

"Only after she was found there."

"Have you ever visited that room yourself?"

"No! I've never had the slightest inclination to visit a storage room at a nightclub. I'm aware that people sometimes went there for a quiet little chat, but I've never done so myself. In my view, one goes to a nightclub for the noise, not a private conversation."

"When was the last time you saw Miss Taylor that evening?"

"She was dancing with an actor from *The Boys from Limerick*. That show's been running for more than six months now. Now and again there's a play that proves incredibly popular and you just can't understand why. Don't you find that? I can't recall the actor's name now, but I told the police about him. Not that I'm suggesting he's the murderer, you understand; he seemed like an agreeable fellow. He might have seen something, though."

"What time would that have been?"

"I couldn't honestly tell you. I'd had a couple too many vermouths for my own good by that point. Then the police spoiled everything at midnight. There really wasn't any need for that. Allow people to have a bit of fun, I say."

A wide man in a dark suit was next to give evidence. He had heavy jowls, a thick neck and small, darting eyes. He gave his address as Rupert Court, Soho.

"Mr Laurence Costello," said the coroner. "You were working as a doorman at Aunt Flo's nightclub on the night of Miss Taylor's death. Is that right?"

"Yes, sir." His voice was quiet, his manner hesitant.

"How well did you know Miss Taylor?"

"Not very well, but I recognised her face. I saw her arrive with Miss Drummond."

"And how did she seem when she arrived?"

"Quite well, sir."

"Not grouchy, as Miss Drummond said?"

"I couldn't say... I didn't know her well enough to gauge her mood, sir. We merely exchanged greetings."

"Did you see Miss Taylor again before her death?"

"Not that I remember. I may have glimpsed her while I was walking around, but I don't specifically remember doing so."

"And you discovered Miss Taylor's body in the storage room, is that right?"

Laurence swept a hand across his brow and nodded.

"What time was that?"

"It was after the police had left, sir. About half-past one."

"Can you describe the storage room?"

"It's a little room, sir. Used to store things."

Light laughter rippled around the room, causing his face to flush.

"Most informative, Mr Costello. What was the purpose of your visit to the room when you discovered Miss Taylor lying there?"

"I was tidying away some chairs. It had been a busy evening and we'd needed extra ones from the storage room."

"Were you aware that guests sometimes used the room for private conversations?"

"Yes, but they weren't supposed to. If I came across anyone in there I'd ask them to leave. Politely, of course. We tried to keep everyone within the two main floors of the club. The upper storeys were for staff only."

"Were you aware that anyone had been inside the storage room that night?"

"No." Laurence's brow glistened with perspiration.

"You didn't see anyone go in or out of it that night? I'm referring to staff *and* guests here."

"No. I didn't see anyone go in or out at all."

The pathologist, Sir Gordon Denison, responded calmly to the coroner's questions in a way that only a man accustomed to encountering unexplained deaths could. He had arrived at the murder scene a little after half-past two. Miss Taylor had been shot from a range of four or five feet and had died from a gunshot wound to the left side of her chest. The time of death was estimated to be around midnight.

Inspector Grover of C Division spoke next. A large man, who wheezed between sentences, he explained how the murder scene had been carefully examined with the help of a ballistics expert. Only one shot appeared to have been fired and the bullet had been found embedded in the wall of the room. Its position indicated that Miss Taylor had been standing when the shot was fired. The weapon was believed to have been a Webley Mark Six revolver, commonly used during wartime combat. The weapon had not been found.

As Inspector Grover spoke, Augusta caught Detective Inspector Fisher's eye again. It felt rather strange that the two of them should find themselves in this place, at this event. She hadn't expected to see him again after the war ended. She couldn't even remember who had told her he was now an inspector at Scotland Yard, but she had recalled the fact quickly enough during the raid at the club. *Was he ever a constable or sergeant before reaching the rank of inspec-*

tor? She doubted it. Given his wartime achievements, the rules had most likely been bent a little.

The murder weapon might not have been found, but its owner had. Billy Kemery was a shifty-looking man with dark eyes and pockmarked skin.

"When did you notice that your revolver was missing?" the coroner asked him.

"About 'alfway through the evening."

"What time do you consider to be halfway through the evening?"

"Dunno. Eleven, I s'pose."

"Some would consider that to be rather late in the evening, but each to his own. Where was your gun kept before you lost it?"

"In an 'olster. An' I'll be honest with you, sir, it weren't no good. I 'ad a better one once but it broke, so I got this new one from a place down Old Kent Road. Can't say I liked the look of it, but I was in an 'urry."

"And the gun fell out of your holster, did it?"

"Yeah, must of slipped out. Didn't know nothin' about it till I saw it weren't there."

"Where were you when it fell out? On the dance floor?"

"I ain't no dancer, sir. I was sittin' at a table."

"And you discovered that your gun had fallen out of the holster at about eleven o'clock?"

"Yeah, about then."

"Did you tell anyone it had gone missing?"

"I didn't wanna start spreadin' the word too much. It might of made people panic. I just wen' and spoke to Aunt Flo."

"Mrs Florence Morrell, the owner of Flo's Club?"

"Yeah."

"And you told her your gun was missing."

"Yeah. She weren't too 'appy about it, but she said she'd get some of 'er chaps out lookin' for it. Only it ain't never turned up, and now it sounds like it's been used in that 'orrible shootin'."

"It does indeed. Was your gun loaded while it was in your holster?"

"It was, yeah."

"May I ask why?"

"Yer never know when yer gonna need it."

"I'm not sure that would be the view of most law-abiding citizens."

"Well, I ain't exac'ly yer normal law-abidin' citizen, sir."

Chapter 17

THAT EVENING, Augusta rested her notebook on the table next to the canary cage and chewed the end of her pencil.

Where to start?

Laurence Costello had perspired heavily while giving his deposition at the inquest. Perhaps the room was too warm for him. It had certainly been crammed with people. Even so, he looked uneasy. And he was the one who had found Miss Taylor's body. That alone could paint someone as a suspect. *Can he be trusted?* Augusta wasn't sure, so she wrote his name down in her notebook.

She considered Cissy Drummond next. *There was no telling with her, given that she was an accomplished actress. Could she have shot her friend in the storage room?* Cissy had been a little too keen to emphasise that she had never set foot in there for Augusta's liking. Although she and Miss Taylor had been described as friends, Augusta had not detected any evidence of great fondness between the two. *Perhaps it wasn't a proper friendship after all.* It seemed as if Miss Taylor had wanted Miss Drummond's help with her career, but perhaps that was just the way Miss Drummond wanted to portray the situation. A great deal had certainly been left unsaid. She wrote down Cissy's name.

Gabriel Lennox had been remarkable in his absence from the inquest. He hadn't been summoned to give evidence and had chosen not to appear in the public gallery. *Inspector Fisher was interested in talking to Mr Lennox, so why wasn't he there?* Even if he hadn't been required to speak, Augusta thought it strange that he had failed to attend the inquest of a woman he had almost married. He had told Augusta that he and Miss Taylor had spoken briefly that evening. *Did he have a longer conversation with her that he wasn't prepared to admit to?* Augusta added his name to her notebook.

"What was the motive for the murder?" she asked Sparky.

Lady Hereford's canary regarded her for a moment before preening himself with great enthusiasm.

Could it have been money? she wondered. Miss Taylor was out of work, but maybe she had been due a large inheritance. Her father hadn't indicated anything of the sort at the inquest, however. *Was it love?* Gabriel had received only a passing reference from Jean's father. Perhaps Jean had fallen in with another fellow. Miss Drummond had mentioned her dancing with an actor from *The Boys from Limerick*. Augusta wondered who he might be, and whether the police had spoken to him yet.

She made some more notes.

"There's also revenge to consider," she said aloud to the disinterested canary. "Did Miss Taylor do something unpleasant to someone? Perhaps someone felt betrayed. Or perhaps she knew something she shouldn't have. Maybe someone murdered her to buy her silence. Some people are silenced because they've threatened to expose someone. Maybe the motive was blackmail."

Sparky lifted his head and let out a little trill.

Augusta dropped her pencil. "Did you just sing?"

The little bird stared at her.

"Oh, I see. You're playing with me now."

He lifted his head again and let out a longer trill, more varied in tone this time. The little feathers around his throat trembled.

Augusta sat back in her chair and listened. "Well, that's lovely, Sparky. Lady Hereford will be extremely proud when I tell her."

Another song followed, then he hopped over to his food bowl and pecked at a piece of apple.

"The show's over now, is it? Thank you for the interlude. I'm pleased you're feeling more at home here now."

Still smiling at the canary, Augusta closed her eyes and pictured each of the witnesses from the inquest. Trying hard to remember everything they had said, she focused on any possible inconsistencies.

Something isn't quite right. Something feels a little off and illogical. What is it exactly?

Then it came to her. *That's right; it's the gun. Something isn't quite right about the gun.*

Chapter 18

Westminster Bridge felt unnervingly quiet to Laurence Costello as he waited beside a lamp post. His heart skipped a beat each time a figure emerged from the fog. He wondered how he could stop himself from feeling so anxious. He had been feeling like this ever since that girl died.

"What you doin' 'ere?" asked an elderly man with an unsteady gait.

"I'm waiting for a friend."

"Strange place ter meet a friend. I'm headin' fer an 'ostelry down by the wharves. Better'n 'angin' about 'ere. Can yer 'elp an old soldier wiv a drink, by any chance?"

Laurence gave him sixpence and the man went on his way.

Cissy Drummond slunk out of the fog like a black cat. Laurence startled at her sudden appearance.

"Here you are," she said. "I thought I might never find you in this weather." The collar of her long coat was pulled right up to the brim of her hat. She had wrapped a scarf around the lower part of her face, leaving only her eyes visible. They weren't rimmed with black this evening. Presumably she didn't want to be recognised.

Laurence's mouth felt dry as he glanced around.

"What are you looking at?" she asked.

"Just checking no one can see us."

"Of course no one can see us! We're standing in the middle of a bridge that's completely covered in fog. Rather handy, wouldn't you say? You haven't told anyone about this meeting, have you?"

"No."

"Not even Flo?"

"She's the last person I'd tell."

"That suggests you've considered telling someone else."

"No, I haven't told anyone. Nor will I!"

"Good."

"Why did you want to see me?" he asked.

"What have you told the police?"

"As little as possible."

"Have you mentioned my name?"

"No!"

"So they don't know what you've been up to?"

"No, not yet."

"*Not yet*? That doesn't fill me with confidence."

"Not at all is what I meant. They'll probably ask me more questions soon, and I'm finding it difficult to lie. I've never been very good at it."

She laughed. "You should have thought about that before! You can hardly have expected to get away with it without lying."

"None of this was my choice."

"I'm afraid I don't have time to worry about your problems, Laurence. I have enough of my own to sort out."

She offered him a cigarette, which he accepted. They remained quiet as a group of young men walked past.

Why am I so scared of this woman? Laurence wondered. *I'm almost twice her size.* He felt as though she were speaking to him as a schoolmistress might speak to a wayward pupil. He instinctively felt as though he should be the subservient one. Although he wasn't proud of himself for going along with this, it felt easier that way.

"We can't change anything that's happened now, can we?" she continued. "What's important is the way we manage things from this moment onwards. Most importantly, no one must ever find out that we're acquainted. Do you think you can manage that?"

"I'll try."

"You need to do better than *try*," she hissed. "You need to be able to handle the police when they speak to you again. They're likely to ask some extremely searching questions." Cigarette smoke swirled around her, its escape constrained by the fog.

"I'll do my best."

Cissy scowled.

"I will!" he protested. "And that's all I can do. But if they start asking me direct questions about things, I know I'll struggle to lie."

"If time were on our side I'd suggest you take some acting lessons. For the time being, you'll just have to deny everything. Do you have a lawyer?"

"No. Where would I find one?"

"You don't know any?"

"Only the ones Mrs Morrell uses."

"Well, you can't ask one of them. Leave it with me; I should be able to find someone. For what it's worth, I think you acquitted yourself pretty well at the inquest."

"Do you think so?"

"Yes. You should be encouraged by your performance."

"Well, I didn't have to lie, you see. It was just a case of leaving certain things out."

"Just carry on with that approach, Laurence. Leave certain things out and we'll both be fine."

Cissy patted his arm and he felt a tingling sensation where she had touched him.

Then she drew her face closer to his and spoke in a low purr. "Now, we need to stay out of each other's way. No more messages from Mr White, I'm afraid. If you find yourself under duress, my name must never be mentioned. Is that clear?"

He nodded.

"I have a heck of a lot to lose," she continued. "I think we all do."

Laurence nodded again. "Mrs Morrell would be very disappointed in me if she found out. She really trusts me."

Cissy laughed. "That's rather foolish of her."

"She's not foolish! I never intended to deceive her."

"Isn't it sad that we do the worst things to the people we care most about? Never mind, Laurence. Just concentrate on what you said at the inquest and keep repeating that same story. Forget about the bits you left out and they'll soon be out of your mind. Before long, you'll be so convinced by your own story that the police won't suspect a thing. But mark my words: if you spend all your time worrying about it, they'll have it out of you in an instant."

Chapter 19

"Back again, Mrs Peel?" Detective Inspector Fisher gestured for her to take a seat in his office.

"I suppose I've got myself involved now." She took off her gloves and put them in her handbag.

"So much for the quiet life, eh?"

"I'm surprised you didn't opt for a quiet life yourself."

"I did try it once." He scratched at his temple. "I tried quite hard, in fact. But quietness taunts the mind, doesn't it? I realised I was happier being busy. My wife and son are a good distraction."

Augusta tried to imagine him with a family. "Congratulations on your marriage, Detective Inspector."

"Thank you." A smile played on his lips. "I know what you're thinking, Mrs Peel. I never was quite the marrying type, was I?" He cleared his throat. "We have a little dachshund, too. Herbert."

"How lovely."

"He causes quite a lot of mischief, actually. Doesn't listen to a word I say. Obeys the wife, though, and I suppose that's the most important thing."

"Indeed."

"And you have your canary."

"Yes. Sparky's the sum total of my family… and he doesn't even belong to me."

"Oh, I'm sorry, I didn't mean to suggest that you were lonely in any way. I—"

"It's quite all right. I've always been quite happy in my own company. You know that."

"Good. Let's talk about the inquest, shall we? What did you make of it?"

"It was quite informative, though not exactly my first choice of entertainment."

"Goodness, no. Not entertaining at all. And inconclusive, as we've been granted an adjournment to continue our investigation."

"I'm surprised Mr Lennox wasn't summoned."

"It would have been interesting to hear from him. However, his relationship with Miss Taylor ended several months ago, and I think the coroner wanted to hear from those who had remained close to her, or who were with her that evening."

"Cissy Drummond was certainly entertaining. Is she a possible suspect?"

"We can't rule her out yet. On the other hand, I can't see what her motive would have been."

"I imagine she's a difficult person to get a straight answer from."

"Absolutely. I've had one conversation with her so far and she ran rings around me. I allowed her to, of course."

"Of course."

"Given that she's a possible suspect, allowing her to think she's in charge is the best approach at this stage."

"Laurence Costello must surely be a suspect, given that he discovered Miss Taylor's body."

"Yes. He could be lying about the whole thing, of course. Perhaps he found her alive in that room."

"Do you think he's lying?"

"I don't know yet. He's an uneasy sort of chap. Unusual for someone of his size, wouldn't you say? If I were as big as him, I'd be quite fearless. Imagine how wonderful it would be to have fists that size!"

"I can't say I've ever imagined it. I don't think his fists would look right on me."

"You're quite right, Mrs Peel. They'd appear a little untoward. You wouldn't want to look like a gorilla, would you?"

"I'd need the face, too."

"Absolutely! And please don't, even for a moment, imagine that I was suggesting you had a face that's anywhere close to resembling a gorilla's, Mrs Peel. Quite the opposite, in fact. I do apologise."

"Shall we return to the matter at hand?"

"Let's."

"Do you know who the last person to see Miss Taylor alive was?"

"Not yet. She spoke to a lot of people that evening and we're still trying to establish the order of events."

"We need to find out who else went into that storage room."

"Yes, that's what we're trying to do. No one's owned up to it yet, but that's not very surprising, is it? Miss Taylor either arranged to meet her killer there or she went in there with him. We need witnesses to help us with that, and we're steadily working our way through them. The benefit of the police raid that evening is that we have everyone's names and addresses to hand! That's a very big help indeed."

"Do you think the murderer knew the raid was going to

happen? With all the noise and chaos of the raid concealing the sound of the gunshot, it makes you wonder whether the culprit had heard about it and planned the murder accordingly."

"That's an interesting theory."

"Who knew about the raid?"

"Just a few of the officers from Vine Street. Very few, in fact, because they didn't want Blue Branch to find out."

"Blue Branch?"

"Blue Branch consists of two men – a sergeant and a constable – who work undercover inside the nightclubs to identify breaches in the licensing laws. Cosy work if you can get it."

"Were they there that night?"

"They were, but the superintendent at Vine Street suspects they've been receiving bribes from Mrs Morrell to tip her off about any planned raids."

"So he didn't tell Blue Branch about this one?"

"No, they were left in the dark. Mrs Morrell can't have been pleased about that! Investigations are ongoing, as I understand it, but there may be some charges brought against Blue Branch. Police bribery is a serious offence, you know. Anyway, back to your point about the murderer perhaps knowing that the raid was going to happen. I'd be surprised if he'd known, as the officers involved were all sworn to secrecy. We can't discount it, however."

"I'd like to know a little more about Miss Taylor."

"I'd say Maud Fletcher's your best bet, in that case."

"She spoke at the inquest, didn't she?"

"That's right. She's a waitress at Lyon's Corner House on Coventry Street. A note from me should help if you want to speak to anyone." He put on his spectacles and grabbed a piece of paper from his letter tray.

"I don't want anyone thinking I'm a policewoman."

"They're hardly going to think that! Anyway, police-women don't get to do interesting detective work. It's an awful shame, really. I think you'd make an excellent detective with us here at the Yard."

"I'm supposed to be enjoying a quiet existence."

"Oh yes, so you are."

"But I shall call myself a private detective for the purposes of this case."

"Absolutely fine." He began writing. "I shall say here that I hereby grant Mrs Augusta Peel, private detective, the authority to carry out enquiries on behalf of Scotland Yard."

"Thank you, Detective Inspector."

"And you must invoice me for your work."

"This is all beginning to sound rather official. I only wanted to help because I happened to be there that evening."

"Very well." He handed her the note. "And thank you, Mrs Peel. I'm very happy that you've agreed to assist us."

"Damaged books are beginning to accumulate in my workshop."

"I'm sorry to hear it. Hopefully this will all be resolved soon and you'll be able to return to them."

Augusta put the note in her handbag. "I must say that I feel rather puzzled about the murder weapon... Billy Kemery's revolver."

"What about it?"

"We heard that it fell to the floor and someone picked it up. But what was going through the mind of the chap who picked it up? Did he decide to shoot someone simply because he'd found a gun?"

"I can't imagine that being the motive."

"Had he already decided to murder Miss Taylor that

evening, and by pure chance happened upon a gun to help him do so?"

"That sounds unlikely, too."

"It's almost too much of a coincidence, wouldn't you say, that the murderer just happened to find the gun lying around?"

"I suppose it depends on the level of premeditation," he replied.

"There had to have been an element of premeditation because the murderer somehow managed to get Miss Taylor into that room."

"Either she went freely or she was threatened in some way. If she went of her own accord, it's likely to have been someone she already knew. Or perhaps it was someone she became acquainted with that evening."

"If she was threatened, the culprit had presumably showed her the gun. How did he manage to do that without anyone else seeing?"

"It would have been difficult but not impossible."

The scenario puzzled her. "So the culprit lured her into the storage room, which suggests it was a premeditated attack. But he used a gun he had only just found. That suggests he'd only just formulated a plan. It seems unlikely that he went to the club that evening knowing what he was about to do."

"It may be that an argument had occurred between the two parties earlier in the evening. Then, when the culprit came across the gun, he decided to settle the score."

"Have you found any witnesses who mentioned an argument involving Miss Taylor that evening?"

"Not yet."

"Have you considered the fact that Mr Kemery may have been in on it?"

"Yes. Our men have questioned him, but despite the

man's disreputable nature he has a reliable alibi for the time of Miss Taylor's death."

"Perhaps he colluded with the murderer. Maybe he deliberately allowed the gun to slip out of his holster so the culprit would find it. Or perhaps it didn't fall from his holster at all. I take it there are no witnesses who saw the gun lying on the floor, or they would have done something about it. Perhaps it didn't fall to the floor at all. Maybe he handed it to the culprit himself."

"That's certainly a possibility. But how do you explain the fact that he reported the loss of his gun to Mrs Morrell? I don't think he'd have been so forthcoming if he were trying to cover something up."

"Perhaps Mr Kemery's gun wasn't used in the murder at all?" She suggested. "He said he was carrying a Webley Mark Six, and the revolver used in the shooting was apparently the same type. But there must still be a lot of those guns about."

"Yes, that's a possibility. If so, it would be odd that the murder weapon and Mr Kemery's gun are both missing, however. You'd think at least one of them would have turned up by now. I think Mr Kemery's gun was used, but where it's got to now is anyone's guess. Our men have been searching dustbins, drains and a nearby churchyard. The murderer must have disposed of it somewhere around there."

Augusta sighed. "It just doesn't make sense."

Chapter 20

THE BARTENDER at the Garrick Club picked up Gabriel's empty glass. "Another whiskey and soda, sir?"

"Thank you."

The fire crackled in the hearth as Gabriel leafed through a copy of *The Stage*. The drink arrived and he reached the end of the newspaper, having paid little attention to anything within its pages. He tossed it onto the table, lit a cigarette and noticed his foot tapping. Restlessness was consuming him at the moment. Nothing seemed to calm him at all.

"Just the chap I've been looking for!"

Raffy.

Gabriel's friend pushed his hair out of his face as he approached, looking decidedly more sober than the last time Gabriel had seen him.

"I have a vague memory of you giving me a lift home the other night, Gabe."

"Your memory serves you well."

"That's reassuring to hear, given that it was soaked in whiskey." Raffy sank into a chair on the opposite side of the table from Gabriel. "I'm terribly sorry to hear about poor old Jean. That must have been rather dreadful for you."

"Thank you. Yes, it was an awful shock."

"The same night you drove me home, as well."

"It was indeed."

"In fact, didn't you tell me you were at Flo's Club that night?"

"I did."

Raffy's eyes opened wide. "Did you see her there?"

"Very briefly. It was rather busy."

"And no one saw or heard anything at the time of the murder?"

"Apparently not. The police raid happened at the same time, you see. We were all distracted."

"And some miscreant took advantage of the fact and shot that poor girl? How awful. Who could possibly have wanted to harm someone like Jean?"

"There are plenty of strange people about, Raffy. I'd rather not talk about it any more if you don't mind. It's more or less consumed my thoughts over the past few days."

"Of course." Raffy held up his hands. "I'm sorry. I was hoping I'd find you here, actually, as I wanted to talk to you about *An Evening Swansong*."

Gabriel felt an uncomfortable twinge in his stomach. "I don't like the serious tone in your voice, Raffy. I need to hear that everything's in order."

"It's not that simple, Gabe."

Gabriel lowered his voice, aware that the lounge was quiet. "Don't tell me it's money."

"It's *always* money."

"But we're all ready to go… aren't we?"

"We're all ready to go so long as we don't have to pay anybody."

"Have ticket sales picked up?"

"No."

Gabriel sighed and looked around impatiently for his drink.

The show has to go on. I couldn't call it off now. There's no possible way I could call it off. He imagined the mockery and laughter from his rivals if he did, and the upset of those who worked for him. They were all so excited about the play. *How could there no longer be a play? If it comes to an end now I'll never recover from it. The competition's too great these days for anybody to slip up. I'd never convince anyone to put on another show again, ever. The man who'd staged* The Maid from the Orient *would be finished!*

The long-awaited drink was placed in front of him. He ordered another for Raffy, then took a large gulp.

"Ticket sales will improve as soon as the show starts," he said, already buoyed by false courage from the drink.

"*If* the show starts."

"It has to start! Can't we ask Beaufoy?"

"You know he doesn't want to work with us again."

"I'm sure the old boy didn't really mean that. Try him again, Raffy. Bring him down here so we can both speak to him."

"I can't imagine him—"

"Can't you at least *try?*"

Raffy sat back in his chair. "All right. I'll try."

"Thank you. I'll see what I can do to raise a bit of money in the meantime. We simply can't call it off. We have to keep going." He wiped his brow. "I'm sorry to be a bit of a bore; it's been a difficult week."

"Of course. I understand."

Gabriel's mind whirled for a moment, then a vision of

Harriet in her shimmering blue dress came to him. He couldn't stop thinking about her. "Have you ever fallen in love with the right girl at the wrong time, Raffy?"

"I'm not sure I've ever fallen in love."

"Oh, come now. Of course you have."

"At the wrong time, you say?"

"Yes, Harriet. I mentioned her to you when I drove you home that night."

"You may well have done."

The bartender placed Raffy's drink on the table and Gabriel immediately asked for another round.

"I can't say I remember much of the conversation that night," said Raffy.

"Well, love has come at just the wrong time for us. This business with Jean… I'm quite certain the police will be after me before long."

"Why?"

"Because I almost married her, didn't I? They'll ask around and end up back at my door. I just know it."

"I don't see why they should." Raffy stared at his friend for a moment. "Good grief, Gabe… Tell me you didn't—"

"No, I absolutely did *not*! But they'll suspect me all the same. Isn't that always what happens? Why on earth would Harri stick around with all that going on?"

"I don't know the girl at all, but I'm sure she'll stay if she cares about you enough."

"I had to write her a letter."

"Saying what?"

"Explaining that I'd once been engaged to Jean."

"She didn't know?"

"No."

"Oh dear. That's bad form."

"I never had a chance to tell her! We only met recently, and I didn't want to bring all that business up just yet."

Raffy chuckled.

"What's funny about that?"

"If you haven't told her much about your past, I imagine you'll have a lot of letters to write to her!"

"This is no laughing matter, Raffy! I care very deeply about the poor girl." He drained his drink.

"I'm sorry." Raffy offered him a cigarette. "I'm sure she'll appreciate the letter. You're a thoughtful chap, Gabe, and she'd be foolish not to forgive you. Look, we need to sort the money out. Beaufoy's no longer an option, I'm afraid, and don't even think about visiting that bookie on Whitcomb Street."

"As if I would! Those days are far behind me."

"Are you sure?"

"I have way too much to lose."

"So what are we going to do?"

"I really don't know, Raffy. You were supposed to be looking after that side of things."

"But you're the manager."

"I know that! But I have enough problems to deal with as it is."

Chapter 21

BACK AT HER WORKSHOP, Augusta pasted a layer of glue along the spine of *Great Expectations* and smoothed on a piece of stiff fabric mull.

Jean Taylor's murderer must have known the police raid was going to happen.

Lying the book flat, she placed a piece of waxed paper between the mull and text block, then applied glue to the mull so she could attach the front cover.

Finding out who had tipped the murderer off about the raid would be tricky. *Surely Detective Inspector Fisher has a better chance of identifying the culprit than me.*

The cover wasn't straight. Augusta wiped her brow and quickly prised it off before the glue dried. Then she pulled off the mull and started cutting a new piece, impatient to get the book finished. She didn't usually feel so irritable about her work. She was clearly too distracted to do it properly.

A knock sounded at the door and Harriet walked in, her eyes languid and shoulders slumped. She didn't look her usual pretty self.

Augusta guessed she had received Gabriel Lennox's letter but feigned ignorance. "Oh dear, what's happened? You look like the air's been knocked out of you."

"Can I see Sparky? I need cheering up."

"All right." Augusta gave a sigh of exasperation as she surveyed the pieces of *Great Expectations* lying on her workbench.

"Sorry," said Harriet. "I'm interrupting. Are you busy?"

"I was, but I think it's probably best left as it is. It wasn't going very well."

Harriet stood beside the birdcage up in Augusta's flat and whistled at the canary. "Have you heard him sing yet, Mrs Peel?"

"Yes, a little."

"I want him to sing now."

"He may be feeling a bit unnerved with you staring at him like that."

"Don't canaries like being stared at?"

"I couldn't say for sure."

"Can we let him out?"

"Open the cage door and see if he wants to venture out."

Harriet did so while Augusta went to put the kettle on.

"He's refusing to come out," said Harriet when Augusta returned.

"Stop staring at him, then."

"I feel like a bird in a cage myself sometimes."

"Why's that?"

"It feels as though Mother's locked me in. I've decided to look for a room of my own somewhere."

"That's a good idea."

"Do you think so? I'm nineteen years old now. That's old enough to look after myself. I'll need you to convince Mother, though."

"Why don't you try convincing her yourself and let me know what she says?"

"Oh, we both know what she'll say. She won't want me to leave home until I'm married. But times have changed! She just doesn't see it, does she?"

"I'm sure she'll say no to begin with, but keep trying. Perhaps I can put in a good word, too."

"Thank you, Mrs Peel. Actually, I came here to show you something." She reached into her handbag and pulled out the letter Augusta had been expecting her to mention. "It turns out Gabe was once engaged to that girl who was murdered the other evening."

"Jean Taylor?"

"Yes. He ended the engagement a while ago. He'd been planning to tell me about it, apparently. It's all come as rather a shock."

She handed the letter to Augusta. It was written in a flamboyant hand.

My dearest Harri,

There's something I need to tell you and it's best done via letter, given the circumstances. I hope you don't mind, and I hope that by the time you've finished reading this you'll still harbour some affection for me. I'd be awfully upset if you didn't. I care about you so very much and truly hope you'll find some compassion for a chap like me who's got himself into a bit of a spot! I've so enjoyed the times we've spent together and hope they will soon resume.

I haven't found much opportunity to tell you about my past, but

I'd like to stress that it was never my intention to hide anything from you. However, the terrible events of the other evening have made telling you about a past relationship unavoidable. I'd been planning to tell you about it in due course, you understand but recent events have forced my hand.

The victim of the murder at Flo's was a girl I once knew well. So well, in fact, that Jean Taylor and I were engaged for a period of six months. We met last year, and after a few months I – rather too hastily, I might add – proposed marriage to her. During the course of our engagement, I considered this proposal to have been a mistake and called the whole thing off in July of this year.

I realise this won't be easy for you to read, and I'd like to stress again that I care about you deeply.

An unhappy result of this broken engagement is that the police will no doubt be interested in my activities on the night of Miss Taylor's death. I can assure you now that I had nothing whatsoever to do with it, and that I intend to defend myself. I hope you trust that I'm telling you the truth, dear Harri, though I shall quite understand if you no longer wish to have anything do with me.

I apologise if my former association with Miss Taylor upsets you in any way. It was certainly never my intention to cause you a moment's distress. I care too much to ever do anything like that, my darling girl!

I think it best that we don't see each other for a little while. Please don't be offended by this suggestion; it's solely to protect you. I don't want you being dragged into this awful business. Once the police have established that I'm an innocent man we shall be together again, if you so wish.

Here's hoping you'll find a way to forgive me!

Yours affectionately,

Gabe

Augusta read the letter twice over. Its tone seemed rather light-hearted considering its subject matter, but that was to be expected from a man like Gabriel Lennox.

"So, what do you think?" asked Harriet.

"He appears to have been honest with you." She handed the letter back to her young protégée.

"He does, doesn't he? Poor Gabe. It must have been difficult for him to write."

"Have you shown your mother the letter?"

"No. Should I?"

"I'm not suggesting you should; I was just interested to hear what she thought if she'd read it. I suppose she's already taken a dim view of the man, and the letter's unlikely to change her mind about him."

"Exactly. If anything, it'll make her opinion of him even worse. Mother's so tiresome. I often think I was born to the wrong sister."

Augusta laughed. "What on earth do you mean by that?"

"Didn't you know? Mother's a twin, but Auntie Dora's completely different. I adore her. It's such a shame she lives such a long way away."

"Where does she live?"

"York. It's in the North, apparently. We went there on a train once and it took a terribly long time."

"Well, you might want to show this letter to your mother anyway, Harriet. She'll probably find out about the engagement one way or another."

"How?"

"The papers will report on it."

"Why?"

"Because Gabriel's right when he says that the police will suspect him."

"But it's impossible that he could have harmed her in any way! Can't you speak to your policeman friend about it?"

"It's up to them to decide who they consider to be a suspect."

"But you got us out of that fine. Can't you do something for Gabe?"

"We're talking about *murder*, Harriet. It's rather more serious than drinking alcohol outside licensing hours."

"So show your friend at the Yard this letter! It'll help us prove Gabriel's innocence. Or don't you want to help him?"

"I can help you speak to the police yourself if you like." Augusta imagined Detective Inspector Fisher would be interested to hear what Harriet had to say about Jean Taylor's former fiancé.

"Why would I want to speak to them?"

"To show them the letter and tell them what you've just told me."

The girl paused and looked down at the piece of paper in her hand. "You'd come with me, would you?"

"Yes."

"All right, then. I'll take this to show the police. I want to do whatever I can to help him. I hope he won't mind me doing it. He'll understand that I'm just trying to help, won't he?"

"I'm sure he will."

Harriet gave a little smile. "It's terribly sweet of him to write and explain it all. I understand why he hasn't called on me now. He's obviously worried about what I think. The truth is, I believe him. It's no matter to me that he was once engaged to the girl. I wonder if he isn't a little upset about her death, though, as he must have cared for her once. I suppose he may still have held some affection for her after the engagement had ended. Feelings can't simply be turned off like a tap, can they?" Her brow creased.

"He was the one who ended the engagement, so I suspect that his affection for Miss Taylor was on the wane."

"Which suggests that some affection remained."

"You're the one he's choosing to court now."

Harriet pushed her lips into a pout. "I should think that he cares less for me than he did about her."

"What makes you say that?"

"He proposed marriage to her. He hasn't breathed a single word of it to me!"

"How long have you known him? About a month?"

"Six weeks!"

"That's far too soon for him to start discussing marriage!"

She shrugged. "I wonder if he still cares for her."

"I should think that he's saddened by her death. But he already decided that he wanted to be with you." *More's the pity*, Augusta thought.

"Should I forgive him, then?"

"What is there to forgive him for?"

"For not telling me about Jean Taylor sooner."

"Do you think he purposefully hid the relationship from you?"

"No, but I'd have liked to have known about her. Perhaps he should have understood that."

"Whether you forgive him or not depends on whether you believe he's done anything wrong."

"Well, he hasn't really done anything wrong. So I do forgive him."

"That's settled, then."

Chapter 22

THE NEWSAGENT on the corner of Coventry Street seemed bemused by Augusta's request for a week-old newspaper and charged her extra for the "trouble of findin' it out the back".

She scurried through the rain with it to Lyon's Corner House. Inside the vast restaurant, waitresses in black dresses and white caps busied themselves between the tables. The odour of damp clothing hung in the air.

Augusta eventually spotted Jean Taylor's former house-mate, Maud Fletcher, at the far end of the room. She was distinctively tall with an aquiline nose.

Augusta seated herself at one of the tables Miss Fletcher was waiting on, removed her damp hat and opened the old newspaper to find a report about Jean Taylor's death. Voices hummed and cutlery rattled above the strains of light music.

It wasn't long before Miss Fletcher approached to take her order.

"Tea and a fruit bun, please." Augusta glanced down

and shook her head in dismay. "I've just been reading about that poor actress who was shot at Flo's Club."

"That happened over a week ago." Miss Fletcher peered down at the newspaper. "That's old, that paper."

"I realise that; I found it on a train. I'd travelled down to the country for a while and hadn't kept up with the news. Have they any idea who did it?"

"I don't think so."

"It's very sad."

"Yes. She was a friend of mine."

Augusta feigned surprise. "Really?"

"Miss Taylor and I shared a flat."

"What a strange coincidence! I'm so sorry for your loss. How terrible to lose a friend in such tragic circumstances."

"It's been very difficult."

"Do you think she knew her attacker?"

The waitress glanced around. "I've just got to see to table thirty-six, but then I'll be back."

Augusta was relieved that Maud seemed happy to talk.

"I can't bear to be at home at the moment," said the waitress when she returned. "I've been staying with a friend."

"It must be extremely difficult for you."

Maud wiped her eyes and nodded. "A constable came in here to tell me when it happened. You should have seen the looks on everyone's faces when they saw him. They thought I'd committed a crime! I had to explain what had happened to my supervisor, and then I took the rest of the day off. Everyone's heard about it now, but people don't quite know what to say to me. I went back to the flat with the police and they took some of her things… letters and so on. They haven't returned them yet, but I think they should because her family would like them. I hope they find whoever did this to her."

"Do you think it was someone she knew?"

"It must have been. Why else would she have gone into that little room with him?"

"Did she ever mention to you that she felt as though her life might be in danger? Was there someone she'd fallen out with, perhaps?"

"No, she never mentioned anything like that to me."

"Was there a boyfriend?"

"Not that I knew of. She was still very upset about her engagement to Mr Lennox ending. He must have realised she wouldn't make a very easy wife."

"In what sense?"

Faint suspicion registered on the waitress's face as if she'd suddenly realised she was being interviewed. "You seem rather interested in Jean, if you don't mind me saying."

"Do I? Sorry. I'm just rather a nosy person. Feel free to tell me to stop."

Fortunately, Maud didn't seem to want to stop. She smiled. "I like to talk about her. I cared about her a great deal, despite her faults."

"Which were?"

"She was untidy, careless and rather grumpy at times. She hated the idea of getting older; said it made it harder for her to get work. She wasn't as successful as she'd hoped to be. She was ambitious, but things never really worked out for her, I don't know why. Maybe she didn't have the talent. I've been wondering if that's the case for me, too. I've tried my hardest to become an actress, but here I am working as a waitress!"

"Was Jean unhappy about her career?"

"Yes, and it made her very jealous of actresses who had

been more successful than her. Oh, the supervisor's looking over. I'd better make a show of writing down your order. Was it a tea you asked for? With sandwiches?"

"A fruit bun, thank you. When you say that Jean was jealous at times, do you know if she ever acted on it?"

"Not that I ever knew of. It was all just talk with her."

"Just talk?"

"Yes. I remember an actress getting a role she really wanted once and Jean was so angry she threatened to reveal some sort of scandal about her so the other actress would be dropped."

"Did she actually do it?"

"No, it was just talk, as I say. That was Jean for you."

Chapter 23

"I MISS GABE," grumbled Harriet as the bus trundled along Shaftesbury Avenue. "I wish he'd let me see him."

Augusta was beginning to tire of the girl's lovesick lamentations. "He clearly feels the need to keep his distance until the police have completely disregarded him from their inquiry."

"And how long will that be?"

"Until a suspect is arrested."

They were seated on the upper deck, open to the elements. Despite a few drops of rain, Augusta was enjoying the view as she looked down on cars, delivery vans and the pedestrians thronging the pavements. Ahead, she could just make out the statue of Eros in Piccadilly Circus. She recalled that its official name was the Shaftesbury Memorial Fountain, but no one ever called it that.

"What if they arrest Gabe?" whined Harriet.

"I wouldn't worry about that unless it actually happens."

"Do you think they will?"

"I've no idea."

"Oh, I so wish I could see him again."

"This business with Jean Taylor hasn't put you off at all?"

"No, why should it have? I'm not completely silly, Mrs Peel. I know there have been other girls in his past. And I know what the theatre business can be like with all those dancers and actresses and what have you. There must be a lot of people about with loose morals, as Mother says. In fact, I've had no end of warnings from her about who to avoid and so on. I do know how to be careful."

They disembarked on Piccadilly and entered the narrow thoroughfare of Vine Street.

Harriet paused as the austere, brick-faced police station loomed into view. "What should I say to them?" she asked, her eyes wide.

"Just show them the letter and answer any questions they might have."

"What sort of questions?"

"I don't know yet, but my friend Detective Inspector Fisher will be there, and I'm sure he'll be perfectly nice to you. Just remember that you're here to show them the letter in order to help prove Gabriel's innocence."

"But what if I answer something badly and make things worse for him?"

"I'm sure you won't. All you need do is tell them the truth. And besides, this is about the letter, not you."

Harriet nodded and pursed her lips. "Of course. I want to do whatever I can to help Gabe."

Detective Inspector Fisher was joined by Inspector Grover, the large, wheezy man who had spoken at the inquest. Inspector Grover thanked the ladies for attending and read

Gabriel's letter before passing it to his companion from the Yard.

"We'd like to ask you a few questions about Mr Lennox, Miss Jones," said Inspector Grover. "Please don't worry, you're not in any trouble." He looked her up and down and gave an appreciative smile.

"I should hope not!" responded Harriet. "Does the letter help prove his innocence?"

"It certainly helps in shedding some light on a few things. Were you with Mr Lennox the entire time you were at Flo's Club?"

"Yes."

"From the moment you arrived there until the moment you left?"

"Yes. Well, we didn't leave together. And we were separated when the raid took place."

"But you were together just before the raid happened?"

"He went off a little bit before that, actually."

"Went off where?"

"To speak to a friend. He told me there was a friend he'd been meaning to speak to, and then he went off to speak to him. The raid happened while he was doing that."

"Do you know the name of this friend?"

"No."

"Did he leave you alone?"

"No, he left me with a woman... an actress he'd introduced me to."

"Where were you when he went to speak to this friend?"

"By the dance floor. We'd walked through the lounge a short while beforehand, and he'd spotted the friend he wanted to speak to in there. So when we reached the dance floor and began talking to the actress, he mentioned that he wanted to go back and speak to his friend."

"Who was the actress you were speaking to?"

"I didn't quite catch her name, I'm afraid. Gabriel did tell me, but the music was too loud."

"Not to worry. You're being extremely helpful Miss Jones." Inspector Grover smiled again, unable to take his eyes off the young woman. "And you were with this actress when the raid happened?"

"Yes. I heard whistles coming from upstairs and assumed they were part of the festivities. I'd never been to a nightclub before, you see. It was only when I saw the officers charging in that I realised we were in trouble. It was all very frightening!"

Inspector Grover nodded. "I can imagine."

"People were trying to hide their drinks, so glasses and bottles were being smashed everywhere. I really didn't know what was happening. I tried to run upstairs, but there were more officers up there. Then I ran back down to find Gabriel."

"He was downstairs?"

"Yes, he'd returned to look for me. Then we were all told to line up against the wall and… actually, I was a little upset. It had all been quite a shock. Then I saw Mrs Peel over on the other side of the room. She spoke to one of the constables and managed to get us out of there."

"I see." The inspector gave Augusta a sidelong glance. "You used Detective Inspector Fisher's name, as I understand it, Mrs Peel."

"I'm afraid so. I was supposed to be acting as a responsible chaperone that evening and I'd completely failed. It was a sneaky tactic to make the best of a bad situation."

"Indeed. You're lucky you weren't punished for consuming alcohol after hours."

"I realise that. Miss Jones and I are both very sorry for our actions."

"Fortunately for the two of you we have more important matters to concentrate on than pursuing you for that transgression." He turned back to Harriet. "So you left with Mrs Peel, Miss Jones. How did Mr Lennox feel about that?"

"Quite happy, as far as I can tell. I think he felt guilty for taking me to the nightclub in the first place. He didn't want me getting in any trouble."

"Have you seen him since that evening?" asked Detective Inspector Fisher. He was wearing reading glasses and had been making copious notes as Harriet spoke.

"No. He just sent me the letter you have there."

"You haven't spoken to him at all?"

"No."

"Then you haven't discussed that evening?"

"No, we haven't seen one another!"

"Have you replied to this letter?"

"No. Is Gabriel in trouble, Inspector? He didn't harm Jean Taylor, I know that for sure. He wouldn't be capable of it. I'm here to support him; to make you understand that he didn't do it."

"Very good. Thank you, Miss Jones."

"Perhaps you can tell us how long you've known Mr Lennox," wheezed Inspector Grover.

"Six weeks."

"And you feel you know him well enough to be certain that he wasn't responsible for Miss Taylor's murder?"

"Yes!"

"Six weeks isn't very long."

"It's long enough when you care about someone so very deeply!" Patches of colour appeared on Harriet's cheeks.

"It would help us very much, Miss Jones, if you could remember the name of the friend Mr Lennox wanted to speak to in the lounge. The person he was with shortly before the police raid. Are you sure you can't remember the friend's name?"

"Quite sure. He didn't actually tell me the name."

"Can you recall whether this friend was male or female?"

"I assumed it was a male."

"He referred to this friend using a male pronoun, did he?"

"I think so. I really can't remember now. What's a pronoun? Oh, I'm being made to feel like I've done something wrong myself now. All I wanted to do was show you the letter!" Her brow furrowed and her eyes grew wide.

"No one's trying to make you feel as though you've done anything wrong," said Detective Inspector Fisher. "We'd just like to know who Mr Lennox spoke to that night. That person could prove to be an important alibi witness for him, you see."

Harriet relaxed a little. "I see. I suppose you'd have to ask him yourselves, in that case."

"Yes, we will. A name from you would have corroborated his statement, but never mind. If you remember the name at a later time, would you be so kind as to let us know?"

"Yes. Gabriel spoke to a lot of people that evening, of course."

"I can imagine."

"And I'm sure there'll be a lot of alibis for him. Including me!"

"Of course. Everything you've told us has been noted down."

"Thank you. I only came here to help him."

"And you've been extremely helpful, Miss Jones. Well

done," wheezed Inspector Grover. "It's been a pleasure having you here to talk to us."

Detective Inspector Fisher escorted Augusta and Harriet to the door once the interview was over.

"I think you should have a look around Flo's Club," he said quietly to Augusta as Harriet marched on ahead. "I'll ask a constable to arrange it."

"But I've already seen the club."

"Not in the cold light of day. It's always useful to revisit a scene, as you well know. I'd be interested to hear what you think once you've been there."

Augusta nodded, then gestured toward Harriet. "I think she's found this a little trickier than she expected," she whispered. "I'd better catch up with her."

Once they were out of the station, Harriet headed swiftly in the direction of Piccadilly. Augusta jogged to catch up with her. "Harriet, what is it? Wait for me!"

When the girl turned toward her, Augusta saw that her face was streaked with tears. "I wanted to help, Mrs Peel, but I've only made it worse for him! You saw their faces. They think he did it! And because I can't remember the name of that friend, they think he was speaking to *her*... *Jean Taylor!* I never should have agreed to go there!"

"You haven't made it worse, Harriet. You just told them what they wanted to know."

"But it wasn't enough! And now they suspect him even more!"

Chapter 24

DETECTIVE INSPECTOR FISHER had been right; Flo's Club did look different in the cold light of day. Its frontage was smaller and shabbier than Augusta remembered, and a new sign displaying its new name, The Chicago Club, had been erected outside.

"Here we are, Mrs Peel," said Constable Adams, who had a high voice and pimpled skin.

"Indeed we are."

"Shall we go in?"

"Sounds like a plan."

Florence Morrell answered the door, her dark face framed with waves of thick black hair. She wore a velvet coat trimmed with fur and her lips were painted scarlet.

Constable Adams gave an awkward cough. "I believe you were expecting us, Mrs Morrell."

"I was." She strolled back inside, leaving the constable to close the door behind them.

Augusta caught up with her as she walked into the lounge. It was devoid of furniture and an unexpected smell of fresh paint hung in the air. "I'm Augusta Peel. A private detective who's assisting the Yard."

"They need the help of a lady detective, do they?"

"I happened to be here on the night of Miss Taylor's death."

The proprietress paused and gave her an interested glance. "Were you indeed? I hope you enjoyed yourself."

"I did. I notice you've renamed the club."

"Flo's Club was closed down by the magistrates for breaching licensing laws."

"But you can reopen under a different name?"

"Yes, I can." She gave a smug smile. "I've run clubs here under various names over the years. And a closure is always a good time for a little refit."

"It looks like it's coming along very well," commented Constable Adams.

"It is," responded Florence, turning back to face Augusta. "I dare say you're quite familiar with the place if you've visited the club before, Mrs Peel. Do you need me to show you around?"

"I'd like to see the storage room if possible."

"Of course. It's just this way."

The proprietress led them along a corridor to a staircase. A short red rope hung from the balustrade.

"Is this staircase usually roped off when the club is open?" asked Augusta.

"That's right. It's quite easy to duck under it, as you can see, but guests are fully aware that they're supposed to stay on the ground floor and in the basement. Or the lounge and dance floor, as you would know them."

They climbed the stairs to a small landing with a single window and a door at either end. Long, frayed curtains framed the window.

"This is an old building," said Florence. "Almost a hundred and fifty years old, I think. There isn't a perfectly level wall or floor in the place. My office is just here." She pointed to one of the doors. "I wasn't here at the time of the murder, or I would have heard something. I was down in the reception box when they raided the place."

"It must have come as quite a surprise," Augusta said, mindful of the fact that Mrs Morrell had been relying on Blue Branch to tip her off.

"It was an enormous surprise."

"Did you visit your office at all that evening?"

"Yes, a couple of times, but only briefly on each occasion."

"Did you see anyone else up here?"

"No." She turned toward the other door. "This is the storage room." She pushed the door open.

Augusta noticed the lock below the handle. "Do you usually keep it locked?"

"We lost the key a long time ago. Nothing of any great value is kept in here, so we didn't really see the need to lock it. I'll have to get a new lock put on it now." She turned on the light and they stepped inside. "There's no window in here. This was once a larger space, but we partitioned it off to create a storage room. I don't like coming in here now, it gives me the shivers. I feel so sad for that girl."

There were chairs stacked along one wall, with boxes, crates and music stands against another. Shelving took up the rest of the wall space. Augusta noted a broom, a dustpan and a mop and bucket on the floor. A broken glitter ball sat on a shelf alongside a stack of tablecloths.

"Who uses this room?"

"Mainly myself and my assistant, Mr Costello."

"There's the hole from the bullet," said the constable,

pointing to the small expanse of wall above the chairs. "Miss Taylor was standing in the middle of the room facing her assailant."

"So the murderer was standing with his back to the shelves," said Augusta.

"He must have been, yes."

"This is a small room," observed Augusta. "About ten feet wide, would you say?"

"Yes, it's about that," said Florence.

"Did you know Miss Taylor well, Mrs Morrell?"

"Not terribly well, but I knew her face."

"Did she ever come here with Gabriel Lennox when they were engaged?"

"Yes, I believe she did."

"And you know Mr Lennox well?"

"A lot better than I knew Miss Taylor. He's a delightful chap. A terrible show-off, but I like show-offs at my club. They know how to enjoy themselves. It's no use having a room full of wallflowers."

Augusta glanced around the room again and felt an uncomfortable tingle at the base of her spine. It wasn't pleasant to think about what had happened there. "Thank you for allowing me to have a look."

"Not a great deal to see, is there?" replied Florence. "I don't think we'll ever be able to use it again. I'll get the lock changed and then keep it locked forever. There are more rooms on the upper storey we can use for storage, though I suppose that means an extra flight of stairs for Mr Costello to climb."

Augusta looked over at the door. "Has the handle been dusted for fingerprints?" she asked the constable.

"Yes, but no prints were forthcoming. We think the handles on both sides of the door must have been wiped."

"And the weapon was taken away," mused Augusta. "The murderer must have kept a cool head after committing the crime."

"It's terribly sad to think that it was one of my guests," said Florence. "We get some rather unpleasant types in here, but I can't say I've ever had a guest do something like this before."

"What's your theory on the events of that evening?"

"I can't imagine my thoughts on the matter will count for anything."

"Just out of interest."

"Oh, I don't know. Perhaps the young woman refused a man's advances and paid for it with her life. An awful thing to happen, but not unheard of. Only I didn't see Miss Taylor with a man. I recall her arriving with Cissy Drummond, but that's all I remember of her."

"And how was Miss Drummond that night?"

"Her usual self: attention-seeking and overly demanding of my waiting staff. But my club would remain empty without clientele of her ilk."

"Any hint of an argument between her and Miss Taylor?"

"None. You're not for a moment suggesting that Miss Drummond is the culprit, are you?"

"Not at all."

Back in the lounge, Florence introduced the pair to Laurence Costello, who wore a tight black suit, the jacket buttons of which were straining at his belly. He gave Augusta a friendly smile, his eyes darting about nervously.

"I'll never forget what I saw when I pushed that door open," he said, "it'll stay with me for the rest of my days."

"What time did you find her body?"

"Half-past two."

"She must have been lying there for a couple of hours, in that case. Was the light on or off?"

"Off." He scratched the back of his thick neck. "I turned the light on, and that's when I saw her."

"So the murderer took the time to turn off the light and close the door. Did he wipe his fingerprints from the light switch as well as the door handles?"

"He certainly did," said the constable.

"Tidied up after himself and left her there to be discovered by someone else," said Laurence. "Totally heartless. I don't know how some people sleep at night."

"Thank you for accompanying me," Augusta said to Constable Adams once they had left the club.

"My pleasure, Mrs Peel. Any idea who might have done it?"

"None. You?"

"None at all, madam."

"It could have been just about anyone. Did you know about the planned raid?"

"Yes, I did. I took part in it."

"How many officers at the station knew about it?"

"Not many. They didn't want word getting out." He lowered his voice. "There was some suspicion that Mrs Morrell was being tipped off, so we kept it quiet."

"I see. How many men at Vine Street station knew?"

"Just the ones taking part, I think."

"And how many would that have been?"

"About thirty."

"Right. That doesn't narrow things down very much, then."

"Narrow things down to what, Mrs Peel?"

"Oh, it doesn't matter. Thank you for your help, Constable Adams."

Chapter 25

CISSY DRUMMOND's address was located in a red-brick block of flats on Langham Street in Fitzrovia, a twenty-minute walk from Augusta's home. Augusta loitered outside for a while, wondering what the actress spent her time doing when she wasn't on stage or socialising.

A large black car caught her eye: a Crossley Landaulette parked directly in front of the door to the flats. Its driver sat behind the wheel.

It was worth the wait when a woman in a fitted blue suit and a wide-brimmed hat stepped out of the door.

Cissy Drummond.

The driver got out and opened the rear door for her. Cissy climbed in and Augusta realised she was about to lose sight of the young woman she was trying to surveil. She followed briskly after the Crossley as it pulled away in the direction of Great Portland Street.

The car turned right at the junction, heading north. Augusta frantically looked around for a taxi cab and managed to flag one down.

"Follow that car, please. The black Crossley up ahead."

The cab driver swerved around a horse and cart, then quickly sped up.

Augusta pulled down the little window between her and the driver.

"Not too close, please. I don't want to raise their suspicions."

"You up to summink?"

"Just carrying out a little work on behalf of the police."

"You a policewoman?"

"Not exactly, no."

"Who's in that car? What've they done?"

The traffic halted for a policeman, who was directing the junction at Marylebone Road.

"I'm just carrying out some surveillance. Please don't get too close!"

"If I 'ang back too much I'll lose 'em."

In his enthusiasm, the taxi driver stopped right behind Miss Drummond's car. The landaulette then crossed Marylebone Road and continued onto Albany Street, passing Regent's Park.

How long will the journey take? Augusta hoped she had enough money to cover the fare. *Might Miss Drummond be heading out to the countryside?*

They turned right toward Camden then left onto Camden High Street.

"Still want me to follow 'em?" asked the taxi driver.

"Yes, please."

"This ain't gonna turn out like them Keystone Cops, is it? Cars speedin' about all over the place, people fallin' out into the road, that sorta thing?" He chuckled. "Make me laugh, they do."

"Would you like it to turn out like that?"

"Yeah, I wouldn't mind a bit of excitement today. Been a bit borin' so far, it 'as. I've just took some dull old girl to

Selfridges. Goin' on about table linen, she was." They continued beneath the railway lines and into Chalk Farm. "Never knew what table linen was growin' up," continued the driver. "We didn't 'ave no table linen, see. Old girl was moanin' 'bout the cost of it like someone was all but forcin' 'er to buy it from the dearest store in London! I could've told 'er she should learn to do wivout it. That's what we done. Nine kids, my mum 'ad. So who yer followin', anyway?"

"I can't say."

"Ah, go on. I won't tell no one."

The traffic picked up speed along Haverstock Hill.

"Looks like we're 'eadin' for 'Ampstead at this rate. Probably where that old girl wiv the table linen lives."

They continued uphill through Hampstead, the suburbs falling away as the taxi climbed to the top of the heath.

"Where does this road take us?"

"Golders Green. We're goin' on quite a journey 'ere. You got enough for me fare?"

"I don't know yet."

"'Ad a bloke get in me cab last night, posh as anythin' 'e was. Got in at Mansion 'Ouse and wanted takin' up west. Got all the way up there – Claridge's, I think it was – and 'e didn't 'ave a single penny on 'im! So I drove 'im, calm as yer like, down Marylebone Lane station and 'anded 'im in. Said 'e'd just 'ad dinner wiv the mayor, an' all! I couldn't 'ardly believe it. Dinner wiv the mayor and not a penny on 'im."

"I hope you won't have to hand me over to the police."

"Let's 'ope not, but yer never know."

The road began to slope downhill again. *Is it possible that Cissy Drummond or her driver have become suspicious of the car following behind them for almost half an hour?*

After passing through Golders Green, they reached a crossroads and turned right.

"Looks like we're gettin' somewhere now," commented the driver.

They passed the imposing red-brick buildings of Golders Green Crematorium and turned into an area of tree-lined roads, neat garden hedges and attractive little houses.

"'Ampstead Garden Suburb," he announced.

"Don't follow too closely," Augusta warned. "We've turned into a residential area now, so the car may well stop somewhere around here."

They followed the landaulette through a little maze of roads until it stopped outside a row of terraced houses with white sash windows.

"Drive past them slowly, please. We mustn't draw attention to ourselves."

As they passed the car, Augusta saw Miss Drummond climb out and walk up to a white gate. She swung it open and continued up the path toward the house.

"So that's who yer've been followin'. She looks familiar, some'ow."

"Turn right at the end here and then stop once we're out of sight, please."

The driver did as Augusta asked.

"Thank you for your help. What's the fare?"

"Two and six."

She handed it over and climbed out of the taxi.

"D'yer want me to wait till yer've finished yer police work?" asked the driver. "As I say, I quite fancy a bit of excitement."

Augusta glanced around at the sleepy houses. "I don't think there's much excitement to be had here. I'll find my own way home, thank you."

He doffed his cap and went on his way.

Augusta retrieved a dog lead from her handbag, then walked back to the road where the landaulette was parked and made a point of looking around her. "Rex!" she called out to her imaginary dog.

There were two houses between her and the one Miss Drummond had called at. Augusta knocked at the door of the first one and was relieved when there was no answer. A young woman at the second house said she had seen no sign of a dog.

The next house was the one Miss Drummond had called at. *She seemed quite at home when she stepped through the gate. Is this a familiar place for her? Who lives here?*

Augusta opened the gate, walked up to the door and knocked. A stout, grey-haired lady answered. Her almond-shaped eyes were cat-like and clearly resembled Cissy's.

"I'm so sorry to disturb you," began Augusta, "but you haven't seen a dog on the loose around here, have you? A Jack Russell, brown and white. I don't know how he managed it, but he slipped out of his lead and I can't seem to find him anywhere."

"No, I'm afraid not."

"I really am quite desperate to find him. Is there anybody else in your house who might have seen him?"

"Edith!" the lady called over her shoulder. "Did you see a dog out there just now?"

"No, Ma," the call came back.

Augusta heard the chatter of a young child's voice from the room beyond the hallway.

"Thank you for your help. I'm sorry to have troubled you." She turned to leave.

"No problem at all. I do hope you find him. Or is it a her?"

"A he. Rex, if you see him."

Augusta walked back down the garden path and called at the next few houses so Miss Drummond's driver could see that she hadn't selected the one with the white gate for any particular reason.

"I have seen a dog wandering about, actually," said the lady at the last house. "Is it black?"

"No, brown and white."

"You need to keep him on a tighter lead, dear."

"Thank you. I will next time."

Chapter 26

"I HOPE HER DOG TURNS UP," said Cissy when her mother returned to the room. "What did she say it looked like?"

"Brown and white, apparently."

"My driver might see it out there." She shifted from her kneeling position on the rug. "Ouch, my knees."

"It'll do them no good to sit like that, darling."

"But I need to play with William."

The little boy placed a wooden block on his tower, which gave a precarious wobble and then steadied itself. He gave a whoop and clapped his hands in delight.

"Surely you can't add any more without it falling over, William," said Cissy.

"I can!"

He found another block and carefully placed it on top. The tower leaned to one side, then crashed into Cissy's lap.

"Oh no, there it goes!" she cried.

"Let's build another one!" he said, gathering the blocks together.

Cissy's mother sat down and picked up her knitting. "Has Mr Reynolds found a house for you yet?

"He's seen a place he likes in Burbank."

"I thought you were moving to Los Angeles?"

"It's not far from there."

"It'd better be worth it."

"Of course it'll be worth it. The sun shines all year round over there."

"I shouldn't like that at all."

"Why not?"

"I like the cloud we get here. Too much sun is bad for the complexion."

"You don't have to be outdoors in it much if you don't like it."

"Stay indoors all the time? There's no fun at all in that."

Cissy sighed. "Are you determined to be perfectly miserable about everything to do with America?"

"Not at all. It's obviously a big and exciting country."

"With large movie studios."

"I still don't see what's wrong with the theatre."

"There's nothing wrong with the theatre. You know I love it above anything else. But out there I can do moving pictures *and* the theatre." She looked over at William and then said, "Have you given any more thought to the idea of coming with me?"

"Yes, and I'm afraid the answer's still no, Edith."

"But you'd love it out there. Why not give it a try for a few months?"

"What would I do with this place?"

"You could rent it out."

"I'm not having strangers living here."

"Maybe we could find someone you know."

"I don't know anyone who would need to rent a place. All my friends are quite settled, as am I. The very thought of sailing across the Atlantic chills me to the bone. I'm staying put, I'm afraid. You'll have to find a nanny for William when you get out there." She put down her knitting and watched the boy for a moment. "I'll miss him dreadfully, of course. You must bring him back every few months so I can see him."

"You can see him all the time if you come with me."

"I'm too set in my ways, darling. You'll feel the same way when you get to my age, although goodness knows where you'll be living by then. Timbuktu would be my guess."

Cissy rolled her eyes and rose to her feet. A deep ache pooled in her chest as she watched William build his tower. She could deal with leaving her mother in England, but she certainly couldn't cope with leaving her son behind. It was hard enough only seeing him once a week as it was. She wanted him to live with her in America. The only trouble was, she hadn't told her future husband about him yet.

She rubbed her brow, trying to push the uncomfortable thought from her mind. She had agreed to the marriage without mentioning her illegitimate son. *How did I let it go so far?* There had just never been a good time to tell Grant about William; it had been a whirlwind romance and Grant was keen to be married as soon as possible, as was she. Cissy was eager to live in California, and recent events had made her even more desperate to leave London.

Will Grant still want to marry me if I tell him? He had already been married twice, and his children were only a little younger than Cissy herself. *Will he understand? Is it worth the risk?*

If Grant broke off the engagement, Cissy's dream of working in Hollywood would be dashed. *Perhaps I could pretend that William is my nephew.*

"Are you all right, darling?"

Cissy had momentarily forgotten where she was. "Yes, I'm fine."

"Are you sure? I was watching you just then, muttering to yourself and rubbing your face. You'll encourage the wrinkles that way, you know, and then that American chap won't want to marry you after all."

"Thank you, Ma."

"Something's troubling you."

"No, it's not."

"Is it your friend who was murdered? I'd be ever so upset if one of my friends had been murdered, but this is the first time I've seen you look bothered about it."

"It bothers me terribly, Ma. But I have to put on a brave face, as you know."

"You do indeed."

"Anyway, I need to get back."

Rain was beginning to fall as Cissy travelled home. She watched the raindrops slide down the car window as Golders Green blurred past. She was in no mood to perform that evening. A little pick-me-up would be required in order for Edith to become Cissy. It had been easier to make the transformation when she was younger, but with each year that went by she found it a little harder to become the woman her audience wanted to see.

She leaned forward and spoke to the driver. "Take me to the chemist on Tottenham Court Road, please."

"Very well, madam."

She sat back and lit a cigarette. *All actresses need a little pick-me-up, don't they? How else do they put on their very best performance night after night?*

As Cissy attempted to shrug off a heavy sense of shame about her addiction, Jean's words sprang into her mind:

I wonder if people would be quite so nice to you if they knew the things I know.

The sooner she could make her escape to America the better.

Chapter 27

ONCE THE FINAL curtain for *The Girl from Bentalls* had fallen, the audience spilled out of the Abacus Theatre and into the damp evening air.

Augusta spotted an attendant in the ticket office and asked to speak to Cissy Drummond.

"You can just wait for her by the stage door like the others."

"I'm assisting Scotland Yard. I have a letter here to prove it."

The attendant gave the letter a wary glance.

"I'd like to speak to Miss Drummond about Jean Taylor," Augusta added.

"I'll go and see what she says."

Cissy was seated at her dressing table in a silk kimono, her stage make-up still thickly applied. A slightly built man in a velvet smoking jacket was sitting beside her. He gave Augusta an imperious stare and exhaled a large plume of cigarette smoke. The smell mingled with Cissy's potent perfume.

Cissy was holding Inspector Fisher's note. Augusta prayed the actress wouldn't recognise her from Hampstead Garden Suburb earlier that day.

"It says here that you're assisting Scotland Yard," said Cissy. "How interesting! Doesn't the inspector want to pay me a visit himself?"

"I was under the impression that he'd already spoken to you."

"He has, but I was looking forward to speaking to him again. Never mind. You're here to talk about Jean, are you?"

"Yes."

"Take a seat," said the man with a lopsided smile. A cigarette dangled from the corner of his mouth as he moved a pile of sequinned outfits and feather boas from a small couch onto a nearby table. "I'll open another bottle of champagne," he added.

The couch was so soft that Augusta's knees were just about level with her stomach once she was seated on it. She felt a little foolish with the actress and her companion looking down on her. It was difficult not to feel intimidated.

"I'm intrigued," said Cissy. "Who are you, exactly?"

"My name is Augusta Peel."

"And you're some sort of private detective?"

"Something like that."

"But you're not a policewoman?" asked the man.

"This is Fran." Cissy pointed her cigarette at him. "He's a dreadful bore."

"Francis Masefield," he said, ignoring Cissy's last comment. "I make all her costumes. Although I spend more of my time letting them out these days." He gestured to suggest an expanding waistline.

"I can always find someone else to do it," she snapped.

"But you wouldn't dare, would you, darling?"

"Oh, but I would." She turned back to Augusta. "Fran's known me since I was a girl."

"Which was a very, very long time ago," he added. "Champagne?" He offered Augusta a glass.

"Thank you."

"I like your hair," he continued. "Natural wave or rollers?"

"Fran!" scolded Cissy. "Don't ask such personal questions!"

"I'm only interested. Mrs Peel doesn't mind, do you, Mrs Peel?"

"She's here to ask about Jean," responded Cissy before turning to Augusta. "Any questions you have about Jean Taylor can be answered equally well by Fran. He was with us that evening, although he didn't come along to the club."

"I hate nightclubs," he said. "Boisterous places. And one can never get a decent cup of tea in them."

"You never drink tea."

"I do at eleven o'clock at night."

"Ignore him," said Cissy. "What do you want to know?"

"I'd like to know what Miss Taylor was like," replied Augusta.

"What she was like?" The actress inhaled on her cigarette. "That depended on her mood, really. She was the up and down sort. She was lively at dinner, though, wasn't she, Fran? Almost intolerable, in fact. She was trying so hard to impress my agent, Mr Shepherd."

"And was he impressed?"

"Not really."

"Did his reaction disappoint her?"

"Undoubtedly. She was in a terrible sulk after we left. You missed that bit, Fran."

"I always know when it's time to bow out."

"Was Miss Taylor ambitious?" asked Augusta.

"She was *desperate*," the actress replied.

Fran burst into laughter.

"She was out of work," continued Cissy. "Do you know much of her story? I don't want to repeat everything if you're already familiar with it."

"I heard she struggled to find work after *The Parlour Game*."

"Yes, The Parlour Curse. That's what she was suffering from. Always brings out the worse in people, an experience like that. She was good company when I first got to know her, but that was about twelve years ago. She soon became embittered; it happens in this business."

"I'm terribly embittered," said Fran.

"Why did you agree to have dinner with her that night?" asked Augusta.

"To help her out."

"Why did you want to do that?"

"She was an old friend."

"Did you owe her a favour?"

"No."

"Did you like her?"

"What an odd question! Of course I did. In the right mood, she was wonderful. She could be witty and entertaining, and there was never a dull moment with Jean, that's for sure. But I'm afraid to say that she was disappointing company that evening. She'd started taking life too seriously. It happens to all women when they reach a certain age."

"What about Gabriel Lennox?" Augusta asked. "How did she feel about him?"

"She *adored* him. I couldn't really understand the infatuation myself."

"Was she upset when he ended their engagement?"

Cissy rolled her eyes. "We heard no end of it!" She turned to Francis. "How many times has that man been engaged?"

"Oh, I've lost count. But I'd be exactly the same if I were as handsome as him."

"You're not the marrying type, Fran."

"I may surprise everyone yet."

Cissy turned back to Augusta. "I told Jean to forget about him and find someone else, but she kept throwing herself at the man. It was embarrassing, really."

"Did she speak to Mr Lennox the evening she died?"

"I don't think so. Is he a suspect?"

"I don't know."

"He couldn't possibly be," said Francis. "Gabriel wouldn't hurt a fly. His only crime is staging dreadful plays."

"What about *The Maid from the Orient*?" asked Augusta.

"A case in point."

"A lot of people went to see it," said Cissy.

"That doesn't mean it wasn't dreadful," retorted Fran. "It was on during the war, of course. The public's expectations were much lower then."

"You mentioned that Miss Taylor kept throwing herself at Mr Lennox," said Augusta. "What did you mean by that?"

"Exactly what I said."

"She was still seeing him regularly, was she?"

"That's what she suggested. I can't say I was very interested in the detail. But I did advise her that he needed to regret ending the engagement, and that he was hardly going to do that if she was constantly at his beck and call."

"The poor girl was lovestruck," said Francis. "I know that feeling."

"I've heard she could be rather jealous," said Augusta. "Was she jealous of your success, Miss Drummond?"

"I'm not sure what you're getting at."

"You've been far more successful than she ever was. Was she envious of you?"

"It's a fair question, Cissy," said Francis. "I'd say that Jean was uncommonly jealous. Her main problem was that she wasn't willing to put the work in. She laboured under the misapprehension that all you need is a pretty face. It worked in the early years, of course; it always does. But beauty fades. Unless you have a face like mine, of course."

"In which case there was nothing to fade in the first place," quipped Cissy.

"I can always find someone else who needs their outfits letting out." He gave her a caustic smile.

"Did you know Jean well?" Augusta asked Francis.

"Not that well. But from what I saw, she was certainly embittered, as Cissy said. This business doesn't suit everyone, you know. There's a lot of competition, a lot of rejection and a lot of champagne. The enlarged egos suffer the most. They simply can't understand why people don't worship them as much as they worship themselves."

"Was Jean one of those types?"

"To some degree, yes. It sounds rather brutal, but she thought more of her talent than others did. Discovering the truth about oneself can be sobering, can't it? That's why I always keep myself suitably topped up with drink."

"I've heard Jean threatened to reveal some sort of scandal about another actress in a bid to get her dropped from a role," said Augusta. "Did you ever hear of her doing such a thing?"

Cissy's face stiffened beneath her thick layer of make-up. "She wasn't that desperate."

"You never heard her make such a threat about another actress? Or to you?"

Cissy glanced at the clock on the wall and stubbed out her cigarette. "I've just noticed the time. So sorry, but I need to be getting on, Mrs Peel."

Chapter 28

DRIZZLE FELL in Wardour Street as Laurence Costello loitered under a striped awning. He threw his cigarette butt into a puddle and watched it fizzle out. His heart began to pound and his mouth felt dry. *Why do I keep feeling like this?* He lit another cigarette and inhaled slowly.

The thudding in his chest quickened as a man in a dark suit approached. His pockmarked skin was distinctive beneath the brim of his hat.

Billy Kemery.

Laurence puffed out his chest and assumed a nonchalant expression. It couldn't have contrasted more with the turmoil he felt inside.

Billy avoided eye contact. He simply stood next to Laurence and surveyed the street. "You couldn't of made more of a bigger mess of this if you'd tried," he muttered.

"I don't know how it happened."

"Course you don't. Picture of innocence, ain't you?"

"It just all went wrong."

"You're tellin' me!"

A taxi pulled up in front of them and Florence Morrell

stepped out. She wore a striking purple coat and opened up a matching umbrella.

"Mr Kemery." Her words had a hostile tone.

"Mrs Morrell!" Billy's voice rose an octave, and he doffed his hat. "What a pleasant surprise to see you this mornin'. Well, I'll be on me way now. Good to see you again, Costello." He gave a little whistle as he strode off, as if he hadn't a care in the world.

"What did he want?" she asked, her eyes narrowing.

"He was just digging around for information. You know what he's like."

"I certainly do. Watch out for him, won't you? He's very good at getting other people to do his dirty work for him."

"I'm always on the lookout for that, madam."

"Good." She glanced up at the building behind him. "Well, here we are, then. Two weeks later than planned, but never mind, we've had a lot on. Shall we take a look around?"

The landlord's agent, Mr Furby, was waiting for them inside. "It was most recently used as a grocery store." He tapped the toe of his polished shoe against an empty packing crate. "But it could very easily be adapted for your purposes, Mrs Morrell. It offers lots of space and the perfect location, of course. Right in the very heart of Soho! You couldn't ask for more than that, could you? All the public houses, restaurants and theatres in the area would provide a steady flow of customers to clubs like yours. I hear Flo's Club is reopening under a new name."

"Yes, the Chicago Club."

"Wonderful, wonderful. Terrible shame about that poor girl, though. Have they nabbed the fellow yet?"

"Not yet."

"How awful."

"Am I right in thinking there's a basement in this building?"

"Yes, let me show you," Mr Furby replied. "Fancy putting a dancefloor down there, do you, Mrs Morrell?"

"I'd like to see it first."

Laurence tugged at his collar as they wandered through the empty rooms. *What's Billy Kemery planning to do to me?* He couldn't decide who he was more scared of: Billy or the police.

Cissy Drummond's advice sprang to mind: *You'll be so convinced by your own story that the police won't suspect a thing.* Laurence had repeated his story in his head countless times, but he still didn't feel convinced by it. And as for Mrs Morrell warning him about Billy Kemery, if only she knew! Shame surged through him as he thought about all the lies he had already told her. It was such a terrible mess.

He noticed Mr Furby watching him, then realised the agent was waiting for him to speak.

"Laurence?" said Mrs Morrell. "Did you hear what I said?"

"I'm terribly sorry, madam. I didn't."

"Mr Furby asked how many guests we would be expecting here each evening. I told him that as you're to be the manager, it would be best to ask you."

"Me?" Laurence's mind went blank.

"Are you all right, Laurence?"

"Absolutely fine. I'd say about three hundred. Wouldn't you agree, madam?"

A short while later, Laurence and Mrs Morrell stood beneath her purple umbrella, trying to hail a taxi.

"Perhaps I should give you a few days off, Laurence. You haven't been yourself since the murder."

"I'm quite all right, madam."

"You don't seem all right. Take some time off; I insist. You do realise what'll happen to me if the police decide to forge ahead with the bribery charges, don't you?"

"I imagine there'll be a large fine."

"And prison, most likely."

"Really?"

"Yes. So you can see how heavily I'm relying on you, Laurence. If I end up in jail, everything will fall to you."

His stomach lurched.

"Don't look so worried! You'd manage perfectly well. Just take a few days' rest and everything will be right as rain."

"But what about the murder?"

"What about it?"

"It's a very unpleasant business, madam."

"Of course it is. But we must leave the police to get on with their work, mustn't we? That's for them to sort out. In the meantime, we must concentrate on our clubs, including the new Chicago Club and the other new one on Wardour Street. These are exciting times, Laurence!"

"Even if you go to prison?"

"I doubt it'll be for any longer than a year. Possibly only six months." She turned to face him. "Although Jean Taylor's death was terribly tragic, we mustn't let it take over our lives. The nightclub business is growing ever more competitive, but with you at my side I'm sure we'll be fine." She gave his arm a squeeze.

Laurence forced a smile.

Chapter 29

THERE WAS little doubt that the spine of *Great Expectations* was wonky. Augusta sighed and placed it on the table next to Sparky's cage. She had been distracted while mending it, and it showed. She was left with two options: take it to Holborn Library as it was or pull it apart and begin again.

"What would you do?" she asked Sparky.

He was more responsive to her voice now that he had grown accustomed to his temporary home. He cocked his head and watched her.

She whistled a few bars from an old music-hall tune and the bird ruffled his feathers. A moment later, he lifted his head and let out a happy trill.

"Well done, Sparky!"

She whistled again.

The bird replied with a slightly longer song.

"I'm beginning to see why Lady Hereford enjoys your company so much. I'll miss you when you return home."

A knock sounded at the door. Augusta stood up and peered through the peephole.

It was Gabriel Lennox.

What does he want?

"This is a surprise," Augusta said as she opened the door.

"Mrs Peel." He removed his hat, smoothed down his red hair and gave her a charming smile.

She refused to be flattered by it but politely invited him in.

He surveyed the room, one hand in the pocket of his pale tweed trousers. "Not a bad little place at all." Then he surveyed Augusta. "Work clothes?"

"Yes. I'd have put on my best frock if I'd known you were coming."

He laughed. "Did I hear you talking to that budgie just then?"

"*Canary.*"

"What's the difference?"

"I don't know. But Sparky's a canary."

"Sparky?" He smiled. "I like that name."

"How can I help you, Mr Lennox?"

"What makes you so sure this isn't just a social visit?" He grinned and she responded with an impassive stare. "Fine," he conceded, "I'll get straight to the point. Why did you take poor Harri to speak to the police?"

"How do you know about that?"

"They told me. They won't leave me alone, and now it seems as though they're starting on Harri."

"She spoke to them voluntarily. She showed them your letter in a bid to defend you."

"Did she indeed?"

"It was good of you to write it."

"Thank you. Someone very wise advised me to do so." He grinned and glanced about the room. "What does a chap have to do to get a drink around here?"

. . .

141

A short while later they were seated in Augusta's living room with a brandy apiece.

"What did Harri make of the letter?" he asked.

"She appreciated it."

"She wasn't angry?"

"She was a little upset initially, but once she'd given it some thought she seemed fairly accepting of the situation."

"That's good to hear. It was rather a tricky one to write."

"I can imagine. It was better for her to have a proper explanation from you than to hear about it from other people, however."

"That's what I thought. I felt I owed it to her, really. And you'd suggested I tell her too, of course. I'd have been a fool to ignore your advice, wouldn't I?" He raised his glass and took a swig. "Do you think Harri wants to see me again?"

"For some strange reason, I think she does."

He laughed. "For some strange reason, eh? You're determined to put me in my place, aren't you, Mrs Peel?"

"Mrs Jones isn't keen on you seeing her daughter again, I'm afraid."

"I can imagine. Oh well, we'll deal with that when all this other business has blown over. I don't want Harri getting dragged into it. That's why I was rather perturbed to hear that the police had been speaking to her."

"She wants to do whatever she can to help."

"When you next see her, tell her I'm deeply grateful for her help but that she shouldn't go getting herself involved. I wouldn't want the police twisting her words."

"Are you worried she'll accidentally implicate you?"

"No! How or why would she do such a thing?"

"I don't know. I just wondered whether that was a worry of yours."

"It's not a worry because I've nothing to hide. What evidence do the police have that I had anything to do with Jean's death? None. My main worry is that they'll try to stitch me up if they can't track down the real murderer. That seems to be happening an awful lot these days, and it wouldn't surprise me at all if someone had gone to the police and mentioned my name. A good number of people in this town have it in for me."

"Really? Why?"

"Oh, lots of reasons." He sipped his drink.

"You were seeing Jean Taylor behind Harriet's back, weren't you?"

He scowled. "Where did you hear such nonsense?"

"It doesn't matter. Do you deny it?"

"Look, it was nothing. That girl Jean… she was awfully imposing. She wouldn't give me a moment's peace. I tried reasoning with her, but a girl like that cannot be reasoned with. I made a mistake in proposing marriage to her, and then I ended things a little too abruptly. I learned that a girl like Jean has to be let down gently, so I agreed to meet with her a few times, but there was nothing more to it. I was simply ensuring that she got the message. I thoroughly regret my engagement to Jean Taylor and feel relieved that I made the decision to end things when I did. I'm no gentleman, and I don't believe I've ever pretended to be one, but I shall always behave honourably toward Harri."

"I don't think you'll have the chance once she finds out you were meeting Miss Taylor all along."

"It's nothing for her to worry about. Really, it isn't! And if she truly cares about me, she'll believe what I say."

"Or so you hope."

"Yes, I very much hope so." He sat back and ran his eye over Augusta once again. "I'd say that you and I are not of a dissimilar age, Mrs Peel. Had we met under

143

different circumstances, we might have rubbed along quite well together."

"What do you mean by that?"

"During the war, for example. I expect you were quite different during the war."

Augusta felt her hand tighten around her brandy glass. *Is he trying to unsettle me?* "I think we were all quite different during the war."

"Undoubtedly so. I've a friend who knows Fisher at the Yard. The rumour is that he was an intelligence officer over in Belgium. All very hush-hush, of course. You're a friend of his, aren't you?"

"An acquaintance."

"How did you come to know him?"

"He's the brother of a girl I was at school with."

"Is that so? Harri told me you were in Belgium yourself during the war."

"I worked as a governess there."

"Why didn't you come home when war broke out? Belgium can't have been a very nice place to be, with the Germans invading and what have you."

"It wasn't, but I was very devoted to the family I was working for. The children had grown quite attached to me, and I was fond of them, too. The family couldn't leave the country, so I decided to stay with them. We had to move around a little, but we weren't too badly affected."

He laughed. "Not too badly affected by a world war? I find that difficult to believe. Belgium's a small country, and there were a lot of German soldiers there. I should think everyone who lived there was badly affected."

"Many people in this country were also affected. Were you drafted?"

"No, I was turned away on health grounds. But I busied myself with entertaining everybody here. London needed cheering up! The men who were home on leave really needed entertainment, and I like to think we provided a valuable service."

"I'm sure you did."

"That Fisher chap, who also happened to be in Belgium during the war, clearly thinks a lot of you. You managed to escape the court appearance and fine after that police raid, after all. Is he expecting something in return?"

"No, not at all. He just happens to be someone I've known for a long time."

Gabriel leaned forward. "Can't you see the contradictions in what you're saying, Mrs Peel? One moment Fisher's a mere acquaintance and the next he's someone you've known for years; someone who's willing to bend the rules for you. I hear you've been carrying about a letter that permits you to conduct enquiries on his behalf. Quite an unusual arrangement, isn't it?"

How did he hear about the letter? Augusta gritted her teeth and tried to remain calm. "All I'm interested in is finding out who shot Jean Taylor."

He nodded. "So you're finally willing to admit that you're involved in the investigation. That's all I was after, Mrs Peel; a little honesty. You make quite a play of being mysterious, don't you? Come to think of it, I've never heard any mention of a Mr Peel, and you spend most of your time repairing books and having strange conversations with a canary called Sparky. You're rather an unusual lady."

"And you're rather an unusual man, Mr Lennox."

He laughed. "I'm not sure whether you intended that as a compliment or not, but I've been called far worse." He drained his glass and set it down on the coffee table.

"Would you like another?" she asked, torn between politeness and a growing desire for him to leave.

"That does sound quite tempting, Mrs Peel. As I say, I'm sure different circumstances could have led to us getting along quite well."

Does he really believe that? Or is he trying to call my bluff?

He got to his feet. "But seeing as you're helping your old spying colleague with the investigation, it's probably best that I stay out of your way. If Harri gets any more ideas about talking to the police, you'll talk her out of it, won't you?"

"I can't stop her, Mr Lennox."

He stepped toward her and Augusta resisted the urge to shrink back in her seat.

"It'll only make matters worse. Can't you see that? You need to keep Harri away from your friend Fisher."

"If she's determined to, I—"

"Talk her out of it!" His mouth twisted into a snarl. "She's just a silly little girl, can't you see that? She doesn't know what she's doing! I adore her, of course, but just keep her away. It's for her own good!" He strode past, making a beeline for the door.

Augusta rose to her feet. "For her good, or yours, Mr Lennox?"

He opened the door. "If only you knew, Mrs Peel." He shook his head. "If only you knew."

Chapter 30

"Goodbye, Miss Jones! See you tomorrow."

"Goodbye, Angela!" Harriet waved at the little girl as she walked away, hand in hand with her mother.

Golden autumn sunshine was peeking out between the clouds. Harriet didn't want to go straight home. She fancied a walk.

Her route took her across Southampton Row and Bloomsbury Square, then on past the long row of railings lining the forecourt of the British Museum.

She wondered how Gabriel was faring. He had told her they needed to put their courtship on hold until the police had established his innocence. *But how long will that take?*

Charing Cross Road was busy. She paused to examine the books stacked up on trestle tables outside the various bookshops. She wasn't much of a reader, but she imagined Mrs Peel would enjoy these shops. *How on earth does she cope with spending so much time alone in a basement repairing books? Such a lonely pastime.*

Women like Mrs Peel weren't usually friendly with detectives. *Why is she being so secretive?* The whole business with the police seemed odd. Harriet had always trusted her mother's friend, but now she wasn't so sure. There was a lot that Mrs Peel hadn't told her.

She turned into Old Compton Street. She had dined with Gabriel at a restaurant around here that fateful night. *Where was it exactly?* Everything looked so different in the daytime.

The streets narrowed and Harriet turned into Ham Yard, where several maze-like passageways took her past pubs, clubs and music shops. It looked like the sort of place that would become quite lively in the evenings. How she wished she could visit the area with Gabriel. *Will that be possible any time soon?*

Harriet knew Gabriel's flat was in an apartment block close by, tucked away just behind Piccadilly Circus. She looked for his car but couldn't see it parked outside. He was probably at the Olympus, but she decided he probably wouldn't want her visiting him there. She would have to make do with a view of his apartment block. It wasn't the first time she had stood there, and she wouldn't stay long.

Hopefully just long enough to catch a glimpse of him.

Chapter 31

"Bɪᴛ ɴᴏɪꜱʏ ɪɴ ʜᴇʀᴇ, isn't it?" Gabriel Lennox said as he joined Laurence Costello in the Intrepid Fox pub. He eyed a group of soldiers at the bar, who seemed to be embroiled in a loud disagreement.

"It's always noisy here," mumbled Laurence. "Less chance of anyone overhearing us that way."

"We might struggle to hear each other!" Gabriel glanced over at the bar again. "And I can't say that I want to be caught up in any fisticuffs this evening."

"That lot'll leave us alone."

"I hope so."

Laurence's shoulders were hunched and his brow was heavily creased. He fidgeted with his hands and generally seemed restless. Gabriel knew that feeling. He offered the nightclub worker a cigarette. He wondered whether Laurence could be relied upon. Seeing him now, Gabriel had his reservations.

"So what have you told them?" he asked as he lit their cigarettes.

"The police?"

"Shh! Isn't it obvious who I meant?"

"I told them what we agreed."

"Good. And just to clarify, you haven't breathed a word about seeing me that evening, have you?"

"I told them I saw you at the club."

"Oh, good grief."

"I told them I saw you come in, and that I saw you with Miss Jones by the dance floor. I couldn't lie and say that I hadn't seen you at all because that would have looked too suspicious, don't you think?"

"True. And that's all you told them?"

"Yes."

"Did they ask you a lot of questions about me?"

"Not lots, no."

"Did they ask if you saw me speak to her?"

"Who, Miss Jones?"

"No, Miss *Taylor*. Stop making me say names! We don't want anyone overhearing us, do we?"

"I don't think anyone's very interested."

More men appeared to have involved themselves in the argument at the bar.

"We can't be too careful. Anyway, you didn't see me speaking to her, did you?"

"I only saw you speaking to the lady you arrived with, and that's what I told the police."

"Good. And there was no mention of me going up to the first floor?"

"They asked me if I saw you up there."

"And you told them you didn't."

"Yes."

"And that you saw no one there other than the girl who was, by then, deceased."

"Yes. Which is almost the truth, isn't it?"

"Yes, good. Now, has that book-repairing chaperone woman spoken to you?"

"Who's that?"

"The one who's helping them but pretending she isn't."

"The one who visited the club a few days ago?"

"Did she?"

"A woman calling herself a lady detective accompanied a constable there a few days ago."

"Sensible-looking?"

"The woman or the constable?"

"The woman." He sighed and lowered his voice. "Mrs Peel."

"Yes, I think that was her name."

"Did she ask you any questions?"

"Only a few. She didn't seem very interested in me."

"Good. It's just as well you're a fairly unremarkable person. I can see why Kemery engaged your services."

"How do you know about Kemery?"

"Never mind. The important thing is that Aunt Flo doesn't find out. You'll be in trouble if she does, won't you?"

Laurence shifted uncomfortably in his seat.

"Now, the problem with the book-repairing chaperone is that she suspects me. There's no doubt about that. I don't think she's ever really liked me. I probably remind her of a chap she had a failed love affair with or something. Anyway, I can tell she's rather sharp. And there's something rather peculiar about her as well. She was in Belgium during the war... tells me she was a governess there. You'd have thought any British woman who found herself in Belgium when the Germans invaded would have hotfooted it back here as soon as possible. But not Mrs Peel, it seems. Makes you wonder what she got up to over there. That's by-the-by, however. The trouble is that she knows Fisher at the Yard, and I think he'll listen to anything she has to say. She's already taken Harriet Jones along to the police station, and that really isn't helpful at all. It's not looking good for me. It's time for us to do something."

"Why do we need to do something if you're innocent? Surely they can't arrest you for something you didn't do."

"If we lived in a perfect world, they wouldn't. But that's not how it works, Laurence. Half the time they're so lazy they'll just arrest whoever looks most suspicious."

"Then they could arrest me, too!"

"Yes. You're equally suspicious-looking."

The large man shuddered.

"That's why we need to do something," continued Gabriel.

"Like what?"

"Listen carefully while I explain."

"Are you all right, madam?" A man in an apron and flat cap stepped out of the Jewish butcher's shop Augusta had been lingering outside. "Are you waiting for someone?"

"I'm just looking for my dog." She pulled the dog lead out of her handbag once again. "I lost sight of him around here."

He grinned. "You thought he might have come in here, attracted by the smell, did you?"

"Something like that!"

"What does he look like?"

"Jack Russell, brown and white. Answers to the name of Rex."

"I hope you find him before it gets dark. It's cold out here today."

"Thank you. I'll have another look along Wardour Street."

Augusta walked on slowly, keeping a careful eye on the Intrepid Fox. A quick glance through the doorway earlier had confirmed that Gabriel Lennox had met with Laurence Costello inside. They clearly had a lot to talk about, as they had been in there for a while. She hadn't realised the two men knew each other until now.

Old friends catching up? Or something more sinister?

Chapter 32

AN HOUR LATER, Laurence shuffled out of the Intrepid Fox and into the misty evening air. Gabriel Lennox had given him a lot of work to do. He wondered if he was destined to be the type of man who was always running around for other people. He did all the dirty work, as Aunt Flo had described it, and cleaned up after them. *How has it come to this?* Perhaps he was too good-natured and eager to please. People were constantly taking advantage of it.

What would happen if I refused? There would be trouble, he felt sure of it. He knew too much. *Perhaps I could go to the police?* No one would ever want anything to do with him again, but at least he would feel as though he had done the right thing.

But can the police protect me? He would need a great deal of protection if he told them what he knew, and he doubted they would be prepared to offer that. *I'll have to run away,* he thought. *But even then, someone's bound to come after me. I'll be looking over my shoulder every day... much like now.*

Laurence had received a telegram from Billy Kemery shortly before his meeting with Gabriel Lennox. He tried to calm his mind as he trudged toward the bookmaker's behind the tobacconist on Whitcomb Street. His mother had told him to conquer his fears by imagining the worst thing that could possibly happen. He was doing that now, but it was only causing his fears to increase. His mother had presumably believed that people were fair and rational. Billy Kemery was neither of those things.

The office at the bookmaker's was lit by a single, dim lamp. Billy Kemery presumably didn't want any bright lights drawing attention to his activities. The low lighting cast heavy shadows on Billy's face, giving him a menacing appearance.

Laurence nervously cracked his knuckles as he stood in front of the desk. He was twice Billy's size, so in theory there was no need to be worried. However, he knew that a handful of henchmen would rush in through the door if Billy gave a single shout. Then Laurence would have no chance.

"We finally get to talk, Costello." Billy sat back in his chair and rested his feet on his desk, his face almost completely obscured by shadow. "Aunt Flo ain't gonna appear from anywhere, is she?"

"No. She doesn't know I'm here."

"Good. I've been waitin' a fair while to 'ave this conversation. Turns out you're a tricky man to get ahold of."

"Sorry. It's been really busy at the club."

"I s'pose I should be grateful you've taken the time out to come see me, then. I think you know what question I've been wantin' to ask ya."

"I think so, yes."

"What's that then?"

"About the gun."

"What about the gun?"

"How did it come to be used in a murder?"

"That's right! Top marks to you, Costello. So… how did it?"

"I don't know."

Billy tutted. "That ain't a good answer, son. Try again."

"He must have found it."

"Who?"

"The murderer."

"D'you know who done it?"

"No."

"Did *you* do it?"

"No!"

"Give it to someone, did ya?"

"No, I hid it."

"Hid it? Why?"

"I was worried Aunt Flo might see it."

"She wouldn't like you carryin' a gun, that right?"

"That's right."

"That's funny, given some of the types she 'as in 'er club."

"She doesn't believe in any of her staff carrying guns. She says it would make us as bad as the…"

"The what?"

"Oh, nothing."

"Gangsters? That's what you was about to say, ain't it? Makes you look as bad as someone like me, does it? Well, I ain't claimin' to be no saint, but at least I didn't go 'andin' my gun over to no murderer."

"I didn't hand it to anyone. The murderer must have found out where I'd hidden it."

"You can't of 'idden it very well."

"I thought I had. I wanted to lock it in the safe in the office, but Mrs Morrell was in there at the time. I hid it in the storage room, but I'd planned to go back and put it in the safe later."

"So 'ow'd someone end up findin' it?"

"I've no idea." Laurence felt a bead of sweat trickle down the side of his face.

Billy shook his head. "This is all a bit 'ard to believe, son. And d'you know what makes it a lot worse? The fact I've been 'avin' to cover for you. There's me playin' the fool at the inquest, pretendin' the gun's fell out me 'olster. They're gonna know I was makin' all that up afore long."

"That's the story we agreed. And you had reported it missing to Mrs Morrell."

"Only 'cause I didn't want Big Terry wonderin' why I didn't 'ave it on me no longer. 'Ad to make a play of losin' it, didn't I? I kept to my side of the bargain, see, whereas you... well, I dunno what you was playin' at. None of this would've 'appened if you'd just kept that gun on ya. Someone must of seen you 'idin' it. Who seen ya?"

"No one. I was in the room by myself and the door was shut."

"Locked?"

"No, it wasn't locked. That door doesn't lock."

"You've 'id your gun in a room where the door don't lock? Nice one!"

"It was well hidden."

"Could someone of been 'idin' in there and seen where ya put it?"

"No, there isn't enough room in there for anyone to hide. It's a very small room. Half the size of this one, or maybe even smaller than that."

"Did ya see anyone else go in or out?"

"No."

"You sure about that? 'Cause your face don't look too convincin' to me."

"No! I didn't see anyone else go in or out!"

"I'm assumin' the murderer's took the gun away with 'im."

"He must have done. It certainly wasn't there when I found Miss Taylor's body."

Billy shook his head again. "And when it turns up it'll 'ave your fingerprints and mine all over it."

"Not if the murderer wiped it clean."

"Why would 'e bother doin' that?"

"He wiped the door handles. If he gets rid of the gun he'll wipe that down, too. It may have our fingerprints on it, but it would have his as well."

"Fair point. I'd sooner know where it is, all the same. It all 'appened 'round the time of the raid, didn't it?"

Laurence nodded.

"So 'ow'd he walk outta there with the gun still on 'im? The police was searchin' everyone when they took down all them names. There a door or some stairs 'e could've escaped outta?"

"The only two doors leading out of the building are on the ground floor, and there were officers stationed beside both."

"Could 'e 'ave got out a window?" asked Billy.

"He could have climbed out of one on the first floor, I suppose, but it's quite a jump. I think the police would have spotted him."

"I dunno 'ow 'e got outta there, then. I ain't got no idea when or where that gun'll turn up, but it's left me with a bit of a problem, ain't it? You was supposed to be my man in that place, and now it's closed down."

"It's reopening under a different name."

"When?"

"Soon."

"That ain't good enough. It's still closed for the time bein', and the gun I lent ya's missin'. Ain't lookin' good, is it?"

"I'm sorry… I don't really know what to say. I told you I wasn't the right man for the job."

"So now it's my fault for takin' you on, is it?"

Laurence remained silent, worried that saying anything else would antagonise him further.

Billy took his feet off the desk and leaned forward. "Is it my fault?"

"No."

"Good. You 'ad to think about that, though, didn't you? I'm worried about you, Costello. I don't reckon you're good enough at this. I reckon it'd be best for all of us if ya just fessed up."

"To what?"

"To the girl's murder."

"But I didn't do it!"

"I wen' an' lost my gun in that club and you found it. You must of used it to shoot that girl."

"That's not what happened at all!"

"Sounds like that's what's 'appened to me. Confess to the police; it won't be 'ard for ya. Do it well enough and ya might even escape the 'angman's noose."

Laurence shivered. "I can't do that! I'm innocent!"

"Sometimes these things 'ave to be faced, son. It's the easiest route outta this, I reckon. You ain't got no idea what Big Terry's capable of."

Chapter 33

A MORNING BREEZE rustled the trees in St James's Park and sent a pile of leaves swirling around Augusta and Detective Inspector Fisher. His stick gave a regular tap on the path as they walked.

"I think Mr Lennox is trying to warn me off," she said. "He paid me a visit."

"Could be a sign we're on to something."

"He was annoyed that I'd encouraged Harriet Jones to speak to you."

"I'm not surprised he was annoyed about that. She confirmed that he went off for a short while just before the police raid and couldn't give us the name of the person he was supposedly with. I bet he wishes he'd got his story straight with her now!"

"He also admitted that he'd been seeing Jean Taylor behind Miss Jones's back. I learned that from Cissy Drummond, and he was unable to deny it."

"Excellent. That corroborates some of the entries we saw in Miss Taylor's diary."

"She made a note of the days she saw him, did she?"

"Yes. Nothing detailed, just his name and a time and location."

Poor Harriet. Augusta didn't like the thought of her finding out about Gabriel and Jean, but she hoped it would put an end to the girl's foolish adulation.

"We've found a witness who saw Mr Lennox and Miss Taylor talking at the club that night," he continued. "This witness is reasonably well acquainted with Mr Lennox, so there's little doubt over what he saw."

"Brilliant! Then it may have been her he was speaking to when he went into the lounge."

"It may well have been. The witness was a little tipsy that evening and couldn't be very precise about the time. Nevertheless, there appears to have been a discussion between them. Not a particularly long one, but it was quite animated, according to the witness."

"Was it an argument, do you think?"

"It's possible."

"Did the witness hear what they were saying?"

"It was too noisy, apparently. The witness was standing five or six yards away."

"It may have been a confrontation. Perhaps Miss Taylor had seen him with Miss Jones and didn't take too kindly to it."

"And somehow it escalated to him murdering her in the storage room," he added.

"They must have agreed to meet up there. In the meantime, Mr Lennox happened across the gun that had fallen out of Billy Kemery's holster. How did he manage that? If he'd just been conversing with Miss Taylor, he presumably would have wanted to get back to Miss Jones as quickly as possible so she wouldn't grow suspicious."

"I agree. Perhaps he went back to Miss Jones and then spotted the gun on the floor afterwards."

"And picked it up without Miss Jones or anyone else noticing?" Augusta queried.

"Difficult, I suppose, but not impossible."

"The conversation they had in the lounge must have been particularly fraught if he sought to arm himself before they met again in the storage room."

"I can only assume that Miss Taylor had persistently made a nuisance of herself, so he decided to put an end to it."

"She must have been a terrible nuisance if he was prepared to murder her for it!" Augusta said. "I struggle to believe that a confrontation about a new lady friend could have led to Miss Taylor's murder."

They paused beside the lake, which reflected the colours of autumn in its rippled surface. Beyond the water sat the grey-stoned government buildings of Whitehall.

"I still think it odd that only the murderer appears to have seen the gun lying beneath Billy Kemery's chair," said Augusta. "Might Mr Kemery have given it to someone instead? Do you think he knows more than he's letting on?"

"It's not impossible to imagine that Kemery and Lennox communicated with one another beforehand."

"Which suggests Lennox planned Miss Taylor's murder well in advance."

"Perhaps he didn't really intend to murder her. Maybe the idea was to threaten her or to use the gun for another purpose altogether."

Augusta sighed. "There are still too many possibilities. You and Lennox have a mutual friend, by the way."

"Who?"

"He wouldn't tell me. But he knows you worked for the intelligence service, and that we were both in Belgium during the war. He implied that I might also have worked in intelligence."

"I wonder who his friend is."

"The friend may not actually be real. But I got the impression Lennox had been digging about, trying to find out anything he could about us."

"To what end?" His eyes narrowed.

"To find something to bribe us with, I suppose."

"Well, he won't find anything."

"How do you know that? He's already worked out what we were doing during the war. If the mutual friend is real, you might want to have a think about who it might be. Could it be Jacques, do you think?"

"How would Jacques know Gabriel?"

"Perhaps he was hanging around outside my flat again and the two got talking."

"Have you seen him recently?"

"No."

"He visited my office a few days ago."

"Really?"

"I wasn't there," Detective Inspector Fisher explained. "He left a message saying he'd return."

"And what will you say to him when he does?"

"I won't say anything. It's all history now."

"Do you really see it that way?"

"Yes. You can't go dwelling on things that happened firmly in the past. It was an entirely different world back then."

"It certainly was. Do you remember the journey we took in the back of that laundry van?"

"With all the dirty laundry from that hotel the Germans had commandeered?" he asked. "How could I forget?"

"Especially after it broke down."

"Don't remind me!"

"And then we had to escape across the fields."

"Was that the time we only had that lump of cheese I'd been carrying around in my pocket for subsistence?"

"Yes," Augusta replied. "I don't think I've ever been so hungry."

"Even though you ate most of it?"

"We shared it equally!"

"Well, I pretended that we did."

"You sacrificed your cheese for me?" she said, surprised.

"I certainly did. I had no choice."

"Why not?"

"Because you're insufferably grumpy when you get hungry."

"I am not!"

He gave her a fond smile and they continued on their way.

"Do you have any more suspects?" asked Augusta.

"I've spoken to Laurence Costello. I'm not sure what to think about him."

"He met up with Gabriel Lennox at the Intrepid Fox yesterday."

"Is that so? I'll make a note of it. My money's still on Lennox at the present time. He was seen deep in conversation with Miss Taylor that evening, yet he claims they only greeted one another, nothing more."

"That does seem very suspicious. It's probably worth us keeping an open mind, though. Maud Fletcher revealed something interesting about Miss Taylor's character the other day. She told me she was inclined to be jealous of her rivals. Apparently, an actress landed a role she wanted and Miss Taylor threatened to reveal a scandal about her so she'd be dropped. It made me think of Cissy Drummond and the success she's experienced compared with Miss Taylor. If Miss Fletcher's testimony can be relied upon, it's likely Miss Taylor was jealous of Miss Drummond, don't you think?"

"It's certainly likely."

"Maybe she threatened to reveal a scandal about Miss Drummond, too."

"Do we know of any scandal involving Miss Drummond?"

"I discovered she has a young child."

"How did you find that out?"

"I followed her to an address in Hampstead Garden Suburb. A Mrs Parkinson is listed as living there in the telephone book. I think it very likely that Mrs Parkinson is Miss Drummond's mother."

"How do you know about the child?"

"I heard his or her voice when I called at the house."

"What reason did you give for calling there?"

"A lost dog."

"Very clever."

"Not especially. It's an old trick I used quite a lot in the past. One's presence can be excused just about anywhere if one pretends to be looking for a lost dog. Rex has been lost for about fifteen years now."

"Poor little fellow. Do you think Miss Taylor knew about Miss Drummond's illegitimate child?"

"It's a possibility. I wonder if her fiancé, that rich American banker, is aware of the child."

"You think Miss Taylor may have threatened to scupper the impending marriage? Or perhaps the banker already knows about the child but Miss Drummond is worried her career might be affected by this scandal? The public wouldn't expect an actress to be an angel, exactly, but an illegitimate child would almost certainly affect her reputation. Whichever it is, Miss Drummond clearly has something to hide."

"Something Miss Taylor may have threatened to reveal."

Later that day, Augusta adjusted the angle of her lamp and surveyed the cover of *One Thousand and One Nights*. She had cleaned it and repaired the corners, and it was looking quite neat.

She had been working on the cover for most of the afternoon without paying much attention. Instead, her mind was consumed with thoughts of Gabriel Lennox and Cissy Drummond. Not forgetting Laurence Costello, of course. *Is it possible that he had something to do with the murder?* Augusta was struggling to reach any conclusion at all. The case had seemed so simple at the outset; so straightforward, in fact, that she hadn't understood why Detective Inspector Fisher needed her help.

But it was difficult to identify a key suspect without knowing the motive for Jean Taylor's murder. *Money?* She hadn't made any enquiries about Miss Taylor's wealth or inheritance prospects so far. Perhaps that was the next step.

Augusta placed the cover back on the table, turned off the lamp and locked up the workshop. Climbing the stairs to her flat, she decided to forget all about Jean Taylor's death for the evening.

The first thing she noticed when she turned the light on in her flat was that the window was open, the curtains flapping in the cold breeze.

Who's been in here?

Then she glanced at Sparky's cage. The door was wide open and the canary was nowhere to be seen.

Chapter 34

AUGUSTA'S HEART leapt into her throat as she dashed over to the open window, desperately hoping to see Sparky sitting on the windowsill.

No such luck.

"Sparky!" she called into the evening air.

London's rooftops stretched out before her. Dusk was falling and she realised the canary could be anywhere by now.

A cold sensation gripped her stomach. *Who could be so cruel as to let a little bird out like that? A poor little creature who is unable to fend for himself? And how am I ever going explain this to Lady Hereford?*

He'll come back... won't he?

Augusta retrieved the food bowl from his cage and sprinkled some seed and pieces of fruit onto the windowsill. *Surely that will entice him home.* She prayed it would.

She considered the possibility that Sparky had already returned and was sitting on a bookshelf or curtain pole somewhere. As she began to look around, she caught sight of a white slip of paper on the side table. A note had been scrawled on it:

Let this be a lesson to you.

Who wrote that? And how did he get inside my flat?

Augusta reasoned that someone must have seen who it was. She would ask the tailor in the shop downstairs. Rushing toward the staircase, she was surprised to encounter the bald-headed tailor making his way up.

"Did you happen to see anyone break into my flat this evening?" she asked.

"No. Someone broke in?"

"Yes. And he let Lady Hereford's canary out!"

He rubbed his brow. "I don't know anything about that, but someone's just telephoned for you."

"On your telephone?"

"Yes. What did you give him my telephone number for?"

"I don't even know your number! Who is it?"

"A Mr Fisher. And he's waiting on the line for you."

A few moments later, Augusta found herself standing in the tailor's hallway with the tailor's small son staring at her, thumb in mouth.

She lifted the telephone receiver. "Detective Inspector Fisher?"

"I'll make this quick so as not to inconvenience the gentleman who lives there. I thought you might like to know that Cissy Drummond has been arrested."

Chapter 35

"The gun was found in Miss Drummond's dressing room," Detective Inspector Fisher explained to Augusta in his office the following morning. "She's being held at Vine Street."

"And it's definitely the gun that was used in the murder?"

"C Division have already had Billy Kemery in to confirm that it's his. He wants it back, of course, but there's no chance of that. Now we have the gun we can have a ballistics expert determine whether it was the weapon that fired the fatal shot that night. My bet is that it was. She's rather clever that Miss Drummond, however. She's wiped the gun clean of any fingerprints."

"Why would she wipe the gun but keep it in her possession?"

"As a precaution in case someone else found it, I would imagine."

"But even if her fingerprints were found on it, that wouldn't prove that she fired the fatal shot. Perhaps she was hiding the gun for someone else."

"She didn't do a very good job of it if she was."

"Why would she do such a bad job with something so important?"

"Between you and me, Mrs Peel, Miss Drummond is rather partial to a drink or two. Perhaps she's inclined to be a little careless as a result."

"But she had the presence of mind to wipe the fingerprints from the door handles and the gun. Why go to the trouble of doing all that and then be so careless about hiding the weapon? It seems a little inconsistent to me. Where exactly was the gun found?"

"In a drawer in her dressing table."

"Did the police find it while searching her room?"

"No. It was found by a member of staff at the theatre. Miss Drummond claims she had no knowledge of it being there. She says it was planted."

"I'm almost inclined to believe her."

"C Division carried out a thorough search of the dressing room and found several other items of interest: three phials of cocaine hydrochloride and a tube of morphine tablets."

"It seems there were a few things Miss Drummond wanted to keep secret, then."

"Absolutely."

"The perfect target for someone who knew all her secrets and wanted to scupper her career."

"You think Miss Taylor wanted to do that?"

"It matches up with what I've heard about her so far. We don't know exactly what Miss Taylor knew about Miss Drummond. It may have been the illegitimate son or it may have been the drugs."

"Or perhaps both. That certainly helps in establishing a motive for Miss Drummond. She's engaged to be married to a rich American, with the prospect of a career in Hollywood. She would have wanted to silence anyone who might have threatened her plans."

"But murdering Jean Taylor seems too great a risk for her to take."

"Even if Miss Taylor threatened to ruin her career? She may have been so scared that she felt she had no other option. The substances she's known to take can impair one's judgement and rationale. Perhaps they made her feel untouchable."

"This will all become public knowledge when Miss Drummond appears in court. Whether she committed the murder or not, her career will undoubtedly be over."

"What a mess people make of their lives, eh?"

"I'm surprised no one happened upon the gun sooner if she had it in her dressing room the whole time. Has it been hidden there ever since the murder was committed?"

"Interestingly, the maid who found the gun swore that it wasn't there a week previously, when she last opened the drawer. She gives the room a quick clean most days and a more thorough going-over once a week. Miss Drummond has been using that dressing room for the past three weeks."

"So either Miss Drummond moved the gun into that drawer at some point in the past week or someone else placed it there."

"I don't see how someone could have placed it there without her noticing. That said, it sounds as though she has a lot of guests."

"I was one of them, just a few days ago."

"Was anyone else there at the time?"

"Only her costumier, Francis Masefield."

Detective Inspector Fisher wrote this down. "Let's pay him a visit and see what he can tell us. We'll need to establish who supplied her with the drugs, too."

"Cissy Drummond the murderer," muttered Augusta. "Is it really possible?"

"Knowing this case, anything's possible. Miss Drummond has already employed the services of a lawyer, which is unfortunate for us because that can make the questioning process tricky. That said, the fact that she has retained a lawyer suggests she's worried."

"It'll be very interesting to hear what she has to say. I don't know if it's relevant, but I have a crime of my own to report."

"Really?"

"A missing canary."

"Not Sparky?"

Augusta explained what had happened and showed Detective Inspector Fisher the mysterious note. He put his spectacles on to read it.

"I'm so sorry, Mrs Peel. Do you think this may be connected to the inquiries you've been making on behalf of the Yard?"

"I think so. 'Let this be a lesson to you' must relate to my investigations."

"Who've you spoken to recently?"

"Mr Lennox and Miss Drummond."

"You must have rattled one of them."

"But would either know how to pick a lock and break into my flat? I doubt it. Whoever it was must have found someone to do it for them. I should have asked my landlord to put a different lock on the door. That type of lock can be picked in less than a minute."

"Yes, I suppose it can. All you need is a pin of the right size and a little hook. Perhaps it was Jacques."

"Why would he do such a thing?"

"I don't know." He tapped his pen against the desk. "Was anything else taken?"

"No. And the canary wasn't really taken. He was just let out of the window, which seems enormously cruel. The poor bird doesn't know how to fend for himself." She blinked back the tears that had welled up in her eyes. *How stupid to get so upset over a bird. He's just a canary. And not even my canary.* "I suppose I shall have to tell Lady Hereford," she added.

"Don't do that just yet. Sparky may still return. We'll ask Miss Drummond about the break-in. She's unlikely to have carried it out herself, but she may have ordered someone else to do it on her behalf."

Chapter 36

"YOU HAVE to tell them this is all a load of nonsense, Mr Briars. I've been set up!" Cissy Drummond sucked on her cigarette holder and glared at the chubby-faced, bespectacled lawyer sitting opposite her.

They were seated in a small, spartan room at Vine Street police station. Mr Briars studiously avoided her gaze as he fumbled through some papers.

"It works in our favour that there's no evidence you used the gun to shoot Miss Taylor."

"Of course there isn't. That's because I didn't do it!"

"But we'll need to explain how the gun came to be in your dressing room."

"Someone put it there!"

"Who?"

"Miss Taylor's murderer, that's who! He needed to be rid of the gun, so he made it look like I did it."

"Are you saying the murderer visited your dressing room?"

"He must have done."

"Can you tell me who has visited your dressing room in the last week?"

"Lots and lots of people. I couldn't possibly remember them all."

"We'll need to write a list and give it to the police."

"That's not going to work, Mr Briars."

"It'll form an important part of your defence."

"It's not going to work because the person who put that gun there must have done so while I was out."

"Are you saying he broke into your dressing room?"

"Yes. I never even saw the gun there. The first I knew of it was when the maid found the thing. So someone obviously put it there during the night, then she came in the following morning and discovered it."

"That means the police need to start looking for someone who may have broken into the Abacus Theatre the night before the gun was found."

"Exactly!" She blew a plume of smoke at him. "I feel like I'm doing a lot of the work here. You're supposed to be the one who comes up with these things. Having chosen the most expensive law firm in the West End, I had been hoping for a little more from you."

Mr Briars pushed his glasses up his nose. "I do apologise, Miss Drummond. There's a lot of information to—"

"I'm being framed!"

"Right."

"You *have* to believe me! I'm your client!"

"Very well."

"The last thing I need at the moment is a court appearance, Mr Briars. Once I've appeared in court it'll be reported in the papers and I'll be ruined. *Completely* ruined! I don't think you realise what's at stake here."

"Oh, I realise all right."

"Do you? Then why aren't you out there speaking to

the superintendent at this very moment and explaining why no charges should be brought against me?"

"Because we were discussing... Right, I shall do just that." He got to his feet. "And the drugs... were they planted, too?"

"Yes, everything was planted. I'm completely innocent!"

"Very good. I'll see what I can do." He walked toward the door.

"I won't be appearing in court, you can tell them that. They can't charge me with anything!"

As he left the room, Cissy rubbed her jaw. Her teeth ached from clenching them in anger. A terrible sense of foreboding gripped her. Mr Briars was hopeless, yet no one else could help her. This was exactly what she hadn't wanted to happen.

How did everything go so wrong?

Chapter 37

"Poor Sparky!" lamented Harriet. "Where do you suppose he's gone?"

"If I knew that, I'd have found him by now," responded Augusta. She clamped a hand over her hat to stop it blowing away in the brisk wind.

"Oh dear. I simply can't understand who'd do such a thing."

"Me neither. I've searched all the squares in Bloomsbury. I'd like to try Russell Square again, as that's the largest square."

"With a lot of trees."

"Exactly."

"And what do we do if we see him in a tree? We can't exactly climb up there and get him."

"I can only hope he'll be tempted down by the fruit we're carrying. He's quite tame, you know."

"He might not like this wind. He's not used to wind, is he?"

"No."

"Oh, poor Sparky! I do hope he doesn't get blown away!"

As they turned the corner by the Russell Hotel, the green expanse of Russell Square came into view. The trees swayed in the wind and Augusta prayed she would catch sight of the little bird in one of them.

"I can't believe Cissy Drummond shot Jean Taylor," commented Harriet as they waited to cross the road. "Have you read the newspaper today?"

"I have. It's very shocking indeed."

"I suppose the only good to come out of it is that I'll be able to see Gabe again, given that he's no longer a suspect!"

"Miss Drummond hasn't been convicted of anything yet."

"No, but the gun was found in her dressing room. Why didn't she just throw it away, I wonder?"

"I've been wondering the same thing."

"If she'd thrown it away, no one would ever have known she'd done it."

"She claims the gun was planted there."

"By whom?"

"By the murderer."

"He'd have to have been rather clever to get away with that."

Augusta supposed someone could have broken into Cissy Drummond's dressing room and placed the gun there. The same person could have broken into her own flat and left the threatening note. She decided not to tell Harriet any of this just in case the person who had orchestrated both break-ins happened to be Gabriel Lennox.

"Should I wait for Gabe to contact me? Or should I go and see him?" asked Harriet as they walked into Russell Square.

"I would wait if I were you."

"But why? It's all solved!"

"It isn't solved, Harriet. Many questions remain unanswered, and we can't be certain that the police no longer suspect him."

"But why would they if they believe Cissy Drummond is the murderer?"

"They may have their reasons."

"Could you ask your friend at the Yard?"

"I could do, but that information is likely to be confidential."

"But Gabe's had a thoroughly awful time lately… and so have I! We deserve to see each other again."

"I'm sure he'll contact you again soon. Give it a few days, just to be on the safe side." She glanced up into the trees, secretly hoping Harriet would have nothing more to do with the man. "Now then, can you see a yellow canary around here?"

"Not yet. Why would someone have done this, Mrs Peel? Why be so cruel to poor Sparky?"

"I'm guessing it's someone who doesn't like me."

"Such as?"

"I don't know."

"You must have some idea, Mrs Peel."

Augusta was tempted to mention Gabriel's name, but she couldn't face the hysterical response that would most likely erupt from Harriet. "I can only assume someone was very unhappy with a book I repaired for them."

Chapter 38

GABRIEL LENNOX STUMBLED out of the tobacconist's on Whitcomb Street and sauntered uphill to the Hand and Racquet pub on the corner. He pushed the door and went inside.

Augusta followed.

The interior was small and there were no other women inside as far as she could see. Ignoring the stares of several customers, she made her way toward the bar, where Gabriel stood slumped with his head in his hands.

She stood alongside him. "Has it been such a bad evening?"

He turned toward her. His eyes were red and he looked unusually dishevelled. "You could say that, Mrs Peel," he slurred. "Are you following me?"

"Yes."

He laughed. "There's no use in pretending sometimes, is there? Would you like a brandy?"

"It's my turn to buy you a drink, Mr Lennox."

"A lady buying drinks for a chap, eh? How very

unusual. Is that how they do things in Belgium? A whiskey and soda for me, please."

She placed the order with the barman. "I'm hoping that if I buy you a drink you'll help me with something."

"Something you'll go off and tell that friend of yours at the Yard, is it? Your fellow spy?"

"That's quite enough of that." Augusta glanced around, hoping no one had overheard. "This has nothing to do with him. I want to know who broke into my flat and allowed the poor canary to escape."

"Not little Sparky?"

"Yes."

"No, not him! That's not on at all. Why's that happened? Have you upset someone?"

"You tell me, Mr Lennox."

"I'm guessing you must have done."

"What do you know about the break-in at my flat?"

"Nothing whatsoever. Go easy on me, Mrs Peel. Things are tricky enough as they are."

"I don't see why they should be now that Cissy Drummond's been charged with Miss Taylor's murder. Surely that means you're no longer a suspect?"

"I hope so. Having that accusation levelled at me has already ruined many, many things."

The barman placed their drinks in front of them and Gabriel gulped his down.

"I began the day with a hundred pounds," he said, "and I planned to double it. I had a good tip about a horse at Newmarket. It was such a reliable tip I thought I could come away with two hundred; enough to pay the salaries of everyone involved in *An Evening Swansong* for the next few weeks. Salaries, costumes and a little left over. I've done it before. I've known the tipster a while and he's rarely ever let me down. But that's it now," he wiped his mouth with the back of his hand. "It's all gone. And to make matters worse, my old backers don't want to be involved this time round. I told them the next show's going to be a big hit... easily as good as *The Maid from the Orient*. But no one will listen."

He called out to the barman. "Another whiskey over here, please! Would you like another, Mrs Peel?"

"Not yet, thank you."

"I blame *The Parlour Game*. Johnny Dill was behind that. He was a well-known name, and no one ever predicted it would fail the way it did. Everyone's become overly cautious since then. Audiences are pickier, and I can't shift tickets the way I used to. Rehearsals are still underway, but I'll have to tell them it's all over tomorrow. There's simply no money left. Delilah Barnet doesn't come cheap, you know! But audiences love her. At least, they always used to. I thought her name alone would sell the tickets for us, but tastes are changing. The industry's not what it was, you know."

"I'm sorry to hear it."

"You're not, though, are you, Mrs Peel?" He held her gaze, his head nodding slightly from the effects of the drink. "I shouldn't think it bothers you at all. You don't like me very much, I can tell."

"I don't *dis*like you."

He laughed. "Well, there's praise indeed! Never one to mince your words, are you? I want to be liked; is that so wrong?"

"No, it's not wrong. But I might like you a little more if you told me who broke into my flat."

"I don't know!"

"Fine. Do you think Miss Drummond is a murderer?"

"Why do you ask?"

"I'm interested to hear your opinion of her."

"I think she must be if the gun was found in her dressing room."

"She says she was framed and that someone planted it there."

"She would say that, though, wouldn't she?" He ran a hand through his untidy hair. "I won't be drawn on the subject any more. It has to be left up to the police."

"And you really can't shed any light on who broke into my flat and let the canary out?"

"None! Why do you keep asking me that?"

"I just need to find out who did it."

"I'm sure your inspector friend will help you with that. How's Harri?"

"She's very well."

"Good, good." He turned and leaned back against the bar. "Fabulous girl, she is. Wonderful. Is she looking forward to seeing me again?"

"I couldn't say for sure. A lot has happened since that evening."

He frowned. "She doesn't know that Miss Taylor and I met up after I broke off the engagement, does she?"

"I don't think so. But I've no doubt she'll find out."

His eyes narrowed. "You'd better not tell her."

"That will depend on what you're able to tell me."

He groaned and clapped his hands around his head again. "Oh, what's the use? Tell her anything you like, Mrs Peel. I've lost just about everything as it is. If Harri truly loves me, she'll have me back. She'll forgive me."

Chapter 39

Look at the state of you, Gabe. What's happened?"

Gabriel stumbled past the blurred figure, heading for the sofa. The moment he sank into it, he knew it would be a long time before he got up again. He pulled his hip flask out of his jacket pocket and took a large swig. His troubles immediately began to recede a little, diminished by the heat of the whiskey at the back of his throat. "It's all over."

He sensed Raffy standing in front of him but was unable to focus on his friend properly.

"What is?"

"Everything. The play. The money's all gone. It's finished."

"You intend to call it off?"

"I have to! It's over! I think I've lost my sweet Harri, too."

He felt his hip flask being pulled away from him.

"You've had enough of that."

"No, I haven't!" He wrenched it back. "Not nearly enough! Can I sleep here tonight, Raffy? I promise I won't be any trouble."

"Fine."

"I'll deal with it all in the morning. I'll get myself back on my feet and face it. But tonight I just need to sleep."

He sank his head back and closed his eyes. The sofa rocked, as if it were being tossed on the waves of a choppy sea. He took another swig. Now the waves seemed to be sloshing around inside him. He gripped the arm of his seat, trying to steady himself.

He vaguely remembered that something good had happened. *What is it? Oh yes! Despite everything, there's something to celebrate.*

"Cissy Drummond," he slurred. "She's the one who did it."

"She murdered Jean?"

"Yes. Which means I'm finally off the hook."

Chapter 40

'ACTRESS CHARGED WITH MURDER!' shouted the headline on the front page of the paper. News of the gun and drugs found in Cissy Drummond's dressing room had been made public.

Sitting beside the empty bird cage, Augusta folded away the newspaper and chewed on her pencil. *Could Gabriel Lennox have planted the gun in Cissy Drummond's dressing room? Or did she place it there herself, pretending she'd been set up?* If so, the plan had gone badly wrong. Her career was probably over, as was her impending marriage. *And what of her mother and child in Hampstead Garden Suburb?*

Miss Taylor might have threatened to scupper Miss Drummond's career, but would Miss Drummond really have risked so much to silence her?

Augusta's mind returned to Gabriel. He still seemed suspicious, but, like Cissy, he appeared to have lost everything since the murder. People would soon begin to turn their backs on him. She wondered whether Harriet would do the same.

She felt a heaviness in her chest as she looked over at

the empty perch. She missed chatting her theories over with Sparky. Perhaps it was the way he had cocked his head and appeared to listen intently. Somehow he had helped her process her thoughts.

She looked down at the notes she had made. Cissy Drummond might have been arrested, but something didn't seem right. There were others who still seemed suspicious.

Laurence Costello had become more interesting to Augusta. He lacked the charisma of Mr Lennox and Miss Drummond, but that would probably work in his favour if he wanted to do something illegal. Despite his size, he was the sort of person who could be easily overlooked. He had appeared to be the earnest, honest type at the inquest; someone who was eager to help. *Is it all a ruse?*

Augusta realised there was an inconsistency with regard to the time he had given for his discovery of the body. At the inquest he had stated that it was half-past one, but at Flo's Club he had told her it was half-past two.

Perhaps it was a genuine slip-up.

It was only a small detail, but Augusta tended to notice small details.

Chapter 41

RUPERT COURT. That was the address Laurence Costello had given at the inquest.

The dimly lit passageway ran between Rupert Street and Wardour Street. Augusta turned in by the Blue Posts pub and stopped at a little door between a Chinese restaurant and a dress shop. A mouth-watering aroma from the restaurant lingered in the air.

She knocked at the door. There was no answer.

After a few moments, she tried again. When no reply came, she began to hope that Mr Costello was out at work or socialising. Hopefully she would have enough time to look around. Waiting for passers-by to move on, she took a pin and hook from her handbag and busied herself with the lock.

A moment later Augusta was inside, climbing a dingy, narrow staircase. She paused every few steps, listening out for anyone who might be lurking within.

The staircase opened out into a small living area, which smelled of stale tobacco. A drab curtain hung across the window. Augusta retrieved a torch from her bag and began to look around the room. Dreg-filled glasses sat on the coffee table next to an overfilled ashtray. The couch was worn, and unwashed dishes were stacked up in a small kitchenette.

Beyond a partition lay an unmade bed. And against one wall, almost glowing in the gloom, was a little yellow bird in a cage.

Sparky.

With an excited flip in her stomach, she dashed over to look at him. There was a bowl of water and plenty of food in Sparky's cage. *Laurence has been looking after him!* She felt a rush of relief.

"He didn't let you out of the window after all!" she exclaimed in a loud whisper. "I wonder if he was ever intending to return you."

She swept the torchlight around the room, looking for anything Laurence might have written. She needed evidence that he had authored the note that had been left in her flat, though she figured Sparky's presence would be evidence enough.

A sudden sound from below made her stop. *Was that the door?* There were no footsteps on the stairs. Augusta couldn't imagine a man the size of Laurence Costello being able to creep up them quietly. *Perhaps the noise came from the dress shop beneath her feet. But what if it was him and he finds me here?* Augusta shivered. She knew she would stand no chance against a man of his stature. *Is he a gentle giant? Or a murderer?*

She noticed a box sitting on the shelf above the fireplace. Lifting the lid, she found it filled with papers. She took it over to the coffee table and placed it down next to the ashtray. Augusta had given the note left in her flat to Detective Inspector Fisher, but she remembered what the writing looked like. She had been required to memorise such things in the past.

The box seemed to contain letters and postcards from various friends, but there was one envelope addressed to a familiar name: Mrs Morrell. The handwriting looked similar to that on the warning note. The envelope was unsealed and there was a folded letter inside. Augusta was about to pull it out when she heard the downstairs door open.

Panic seized her. She flung the lid back onto the box, dashed over to the shelf and placed it back where she had found it.

Footsteps sounded on the stairs as she looked around, desperate for somewhere to hide. She dashed behind the couch, crouched down on the gritty floorboards and turned off her torch.

Slow, heavy steps followed. It took him a while to make the climb.

Augusta cautiously peered out from her hiding place and felt a sickening lurch in her stomach as she noticed something white on the coffee table. It was the letter addressed to Mrs Morrell. She had intended to take it with her, but now it was too late.

She retreated back behind the couch just as Laurence stepped into the room. The light turned on and he stopped in his tracks.

Augusta's heart thudded in her mouth. She breathed as slowly as possible in a bid to calm it.

"Hello?" Laurence called out. "Who's here?"

She closed her eyes, her body quivering. *This was such a foolish idea. Why did I ever assume he'd be out all evening?*

The floorboards creaked as he stepped further into the room.

"I know there's someone here," he said. "Show yourself!"

She tried to hold her breath, praying he would give up on the idea that someone had entered his flat. But she knew it was a futile thought. He had undoubtedly seen the letter on the coffee table.

He began to pace around the room. The floorboards creaked as he moved and she heard furniture being scraped across the floor. *It won't be long before he moves the couch. He won't give up until he finds me here.*

"It's me," Augusta announced, scrambling out of her hiding place. She held her arms aloft to show that she was holding no weapon and had no intention of hurting him. "I just came to fetch Sparky."

The man was even larger than she remembered. Her mouth felt dry.

He stared back at her, his jaw hanging down, but his chubby face looked tired rather than angry.

"Sparky?" he said.

"The canary. You broke into my flat and took him, so I decided to do the same."

"How did you get in here?"

"The same way you got into my flat. Can I please take Sparky back now?"

His arms hung loosely by his sides. There was no sign that he was preparing to attack her. Not yet, anyway.

"What have you taken?" he demanded.

"Nothing. I'm just here for the bird. He's not even mine; he belongs to Lady Hereford."

He picked up the envelope from the table. "What's this doing here?"

"I've no idea."

"Did you get it out of that box over there?"

"No," she lied.

He walked over to the box. "It's been moved. You moved it and took this letter out."

"All right, I did. I wanted to see if your handwriting matched the note you left in my flat when you stole Sparky."

"I didn't leave a note."

"The handwriting on the note matches the writing on that envelope."

"Did you read the letter inside that envelope?"

"No."

"Are you telling the truth now?" His small eyes glared sharply.

"Yes, I can honestly say that I am. I can't deny that I would have read it if you hadn't returned when you did, but I didn't have time."

"Good." He grasped the envelope protectively.

What does the letter say? It's clearly important to him.

"Who ordered you to break into my flat?" she asked.

"You know I can't tell you that."

"Was it Jean Taylor's murderer?"

"I have no idea who murdered her."

"The person who took Sparky and left the note was trying to warn me off. He didn't want me investigating Miss Taylor's death. Who are you protecting, Mr Costello?"

"I only did what I was asked to do. Reluctantly, I should add."

"Is it Cissy Drummond?"

"I can't say."

"I think you'd better tell the police everything you know."

"It's too dangerous." His eyes grew wide, as if he were afraid of something.

"Explain that to them. Tell them you're in fear for your life and—"

"But I'm not in fear for my life!"

"Then what could be more important than telling the police who was responsible for the shooting of an innocent girl? If you tell me what you know, I won't tell anyone you stole Lady Hereford's canary."

"I can't." His face hardened and his fists clenched. "Now leave my flat!"

"I'm not leaving without Sparky." Augusta heard her voice waver.

"Fine. Take him!"

She walked over to the cage. "Thank you for looking after him. Can I take the cage as well? It'll be rather difficult to transport him otherwise."

"Yes." Laurence jutted out his jaw. "Now leave!"

Augusta had no desire to antagonise him any further. She carried the cage past him, then turned when she reached the door. "Detective Inspector Fisher would protect you if you told him—"

"No one can protect me! Now get out!"

Augusta hurried out through the door without looking back.

Chapter 42

Augusta kept herself busy in her workshop the following day. The encounter with Laurence had left her feeling unsettled. *How can he be persuaded to talk?* She didn't relish the idea of trying again herself.

Checking her watch, she saw that only ten minutes had passed since she had last visited Sparky up in her flat. Although it was unlikely that anyone would try to take him again, she couldn't be certain and felt the need to check on him regularly. Thankfully, Lady Hereford would never know anything about his kidnap. Augusta didn't like the thought of handing him back when Lady Hereford's hospital stay came to an end.

After a quick search through her workshop drawers, she found some cloth that matched the cover of *One Thousand and One Nights*. The spine on the old book was too ripped to repair, so she would have to use the cloth to make a new one. She was just starting to measure it when a knock sounded at the door and Harriet stepped in, her brow furrowed.

"Is everything all right?"

"Not really." The girl looked around for somewhere to sit before perching herself on a workbench. "It's Gabe."

"Oh?"

"He met me after school yesterday and told me everything. And I truly mean *everything*."

Has he confessed? Maybe he framed Cissy Drummond after all and now feels horribly guilty about it.

"What exactly is *everything*?" asked Augusta.

"All that business with Jean Taylor. How they were still…" she gave a loud gulp, "seeing each other! He told me he didn't love her any more, but that it had taken some time to end the engagement. She wouldn't accept it, you see, and she kept pestering him day after day. He never loved her the way he loves me. He actually told me he loved me. Can you believe that?"

Augusta resisted the temptation to roll her eyes. "And you believe him?"

"Of course I do! I could tell that he meant it. Then he told me he's ruined financially. *An Evening Swansong* isn't going ahead and he's stepped down as manager of the Olympus Theatre. He told me he hasn't a penny to his name."

Augusta wondered how truthful Mr Lennox had really been. "Did he mention his gambling?"

"Oh, yes! He says it's had a real grip on him. He was quite good at it before, you see, and made a lot of money. But then his luck turned and he couldn't make the same amount any more. He feels so terribly bad about letting all those people at the theatre down. He says no one will ever want to work with him again. Can you imagine what that must be like?"

"No."

"He'll have to do something else entirely with his life now, and he really doesn't know what. In fact, he's thinking of moving to Paris. He has a good friend there who's offered to pay for his travel."

"Paris?"

"Yes." A smile crept across Harriet's face. "And he's asked me to go with him."

"When?"

"As soon as possible."

"But he can't do that!"

"Why not?"

"He has no money. And he has no right to go snatching you away like that."

"He's not snatching me. I want to go!"

"Does he intend to marry you?"

"You're beginning to sound like my mother, Mrs Peel."

"I don't suppose you've told her about your Paris plans, have you?"

"No, I haven't. But I'm nineteen, and I can do what I like!"

"Do you really think it's a good idea to run off to Paris with a man who has no work, no money and a gambling habit?"

"His gambling days are far behind him now."

"And you've forgiven him for seeing Miss Taylor behind your back, have you?"

"Now that he's explained it all, I have."

Gabriel was certainly a smooth talker. Augusta shook her head in dismay.

"Do you disapprove?" asked Harriet sullenly.

"I wouldn't say that. I just don't trust the man."

"Why not?"

"Because there are still questions over his involvement in Miss Taylor's death."

"What questions? Everyone, including the police, believe that Cissy Drummond killed her. Gabe is entirely innocent! He had nothing to do with it!"

"So he didn't plant the gun in her dressing room?"

The girl's face was incredulous. "How on earth would he do that?"

"He may have asked someone else to do it. Laurence Costello, perhaps."

"Who's that?"

"He's the man who found Miss Taylor's body in the storage room. I think the pair of them are in this together. Mr Costello broke into my flat and took Sparky."

"Why?"

"Because he wanted to stop me investigating Miss Taylor's death. But do you know what I think? I think someone else asked him to do it. And I think that person is Gabriel Lennox."

"Gabe asked him to steal Sparky?" Harriet's voice was shrill. She got to her feet. "What nonsense, Mrs Peel. You have no idea what you're talking about!"

"It isn't nonsense, and I'm extremely close to finding the evidence I need. Take my advice, Harriet, and stay well away from that man."

The girl's lower lip began to tremble. "You're utterly hateful, Mrs Peel!"

"I'm just trying to help you see sense."

"No, you're not! You're determined to despise him and keep me away from him. But let me tell you something, I'm in love with the man! More in love than I've ever been with anyone. Gabe and I are in love, and there's nothing anyone can do about it! I thought for a while that you might understand because you're a little different to the others. But I was wrong. You're just the same as Mother!"

Augusta watched Harriet leave, slamming the door shut behind her.

If Gabriel Lennox intended to flee to France, Detective Inspector Fisher needed to know about it right away.

Chapter 43

DETECTOR INSPECTOR FISHER was not alone when Augusta arrived at Scotland Yard. Florence Morrell sat at his desk wearing a black, fur-trimmed coat and a black hat. She had a sombre expression on her face, and Augusta immediately deduced that someone had died.

"Laurence Costello jumped to his death from Hungerford Bridge last night," confirmed the detective inspector.

Augusta sat down and took a deep breath. "How awful."

"Someone on the bridge tried to stop him, but he jumped anyway. His body was recovered near Wapping at first light this morning."

"He spoke to me just before he did it," Mrs Morrell added. "He wanted to hand-deliver a letter."

Her eyes shifted to an envelope on the desk. It was the one Augusta had found in the box at his flat.

"What does it say?" asked Augusta.

"It's a confession," replied the nightclub owner, "although he also told me what it said. He's admitted to a number of things I knew nothing about. It seems he was involved in the selling of drugs. If I'd known…" She shook her head and looked down at her hands, which were fidgeting with a handkerchief.

"He was dealing drugs?"

Mrs Morrell nodded. "Cocaine. To the guests in my club. And to think that I trusted him!"

"He was recruited by Billy Kemery," said Detective Inspector Fisher.

Mrs Morrell's eyes grew damp. "He told me they made him do it. He tried to say no, but they wouldn't let him. I told him he should have come to me sooner. I could have sorted it out for him. Silly boy!" Her voice cracked. "His problem was that he always wanted to please people. I never should have employed him; he was far too nice to work at my club. Cissy Drummond was probably one of his customers. She often wanted to speak to him about something. Sometimes she said she had a message to pass on. I assumed they were acquaintances, but I think I understand the real reason now.

"He was terribly distressed when he visited me. He said he thought it best if he didn't work for me any more. I didn't really want to lose him. He was a good worker and I'd asked him to help run my new club. But I was quite upset, so I told him his confession had come as a shock and that I needed time to think about it. I told him to go home and get some rest, and then we would discuss it in the morning. I had no idea he would go and do something like this. No idea at all! I wish I'd kept an eye on him. I should have made him stay at my flat."

"You weren't to know," said the detective inspector.

"I was rather angry at the time. He might still be here now if I hadn't been."

"Your reaction was entirely understandable, Mrs Morrell. He'd betrayed your trust."

"I just wish I hadn't been so angry! I did calm down a bit, and the mood between us was good by the time he left. I refused to accept his resignation, so he knew there was still an opportunity to work for me in some way or another. I didn't know what to think; I just needed time. I barely slept a wink last night."

"We have no idea what sort of pressure he was under from Kemery," said Detective Inspector Fisher. "He and his boss, Terry Gallagher, are very unpleasant types indeed. Perhaps we'll never know the full extent of what he was mixed up in. We'll get Kemery in to answer some questions, though. He clearly didn't tell the truth at the inquest, and now we know why." He turned to Augusta. "Costello admitted to Mrs Morrell that the gun used to shoot Miss Taylor belonged to him."

"It wasn't Billy Kemery's?" asked Augusta.

"It was once Kemery's, but he'd given the gun to Costello. Costello maintains in his letter that he was pressured to accept the gun. He feared the consequences if he refused. Being of a fairly harmless nature, Costello had encountered some clients who, for want of a better expression, had taken advantage of him. He had allowed them to accumulate rather substantial drug debts. Kemery decided to give him a gun to make people think twice before exploiting the man's soft nature."

Mrs Morrell shook her head. "He knew how I felt about guns in my club, and that's why he kept it hidden from me. I can't imagine him ever using one, to be quite honest!"

"So Mr Kemery's story that the gun fell out of his holster was a complete lie?" said Augusta.

"It was indeed," replied Detective Inspector Fisher. "That's probably why the story never sat quite right with you, Mrs Peel."

"He told me he'd planned to put the gun in the safe," said Mrs Morrell. "But I was in the office at the time, so he decided to hide it in the storage room until he could get into the office without me seeing him."

"So Miss Taylor's murderer found the gun in the storage room?" asked Augusta.

"He must have done," responded the detective inspector. "Costello says he hid it inside a box of menu cards. The box was on the floor with the cards strewn about the place when he discovered Miss Taylor's body. Realising he'd be in trouble because his gun had been used, he tidied up the box and the cards."

"So he interfered with the crime scene before summoning the police," commented Augusta. "But how do we know he wasn't just tidying up after carrying out the deed himself?"

"We don't know that for certain."

The story was still frustratingly incomplete.

"If Laurence didn't murder Miss Taylor," said Augusta, "the murderer had to have known he'd put the gun in the box. The murderer somehow knew the gun was there and deliberately lured Miss Taylor into the storage room."

"That seems to be the case, based on Costello's admissions," said the detective inspector.

"I also saw Mr Costello yesterday evening," Augusta confessed.

"Really?"

"Yes. Before he went to see Mrs Morrell. I recovered Sparky from his flat."

"You mean Sparky wasn't lost after all?"

"No, he'd just been stolen. Mr Costello looked after him very well, actually." Her voice became a little choked. "I'm grateful to him for that."

"Even if he did steal the bird in the first place."

"Yes, and I believe he also wrote the note warning me to stay away from the investigation. He wouldn't tell me who had ordered him to do so, though."

"Protecting others until the very end, I see. He also made a further confession. He told Mrs Morrell he'd broken into Cissy Drummond's dressing room at the Abacus Theatre and placed the gun in the drawer."

"Did he say who'd told him to do it?"

"No."

"I asked him," said Mrs Morrell, "but he wouldn't tell me."

"Too frightened to say?" wondered Augusta.

"Or too loyal," replied Detective Inspector Fisher.

"He must have had a good idea who the murderer was," said Augusta. "If only he'd told someone! Keeping it a secret undoubtedly led to his death. He must have just found it all too much to bear."

"Perhaps he felt he'd said too much and that's why he jumped from the bridge," said Mrs Morrell. "He wanted to confess everything he'd done wrong but couldn't quite bring himself to name names. I'd told him to go to the police in the morning and he said he would. I made the mistake of believing him."

"You did your best, Mrs Morrell," said Detective Inspector Fisher. "And we not only have your word for it, but he also wrote it down in his letter. We'll go through it all again in detail later. Hopefully it'll take us a step closer to finding out who the murderer is."

It was hard for Augusta to believe Laurence Costello was really gone. He had ended his life only a few hours after she had broken into his flat.

"If Mr Costello admitted to framing Cissy Drummond, that means she's innocent of Miss Taylor's murder," she said. "You may be interested to know that Gabriel Lennox is planning to travel to Paris, by the way. If you ask me, I think he's running away."

"He must be stopped!" said Detective Inspector Fisher. "I'll alert C Division right away."

"Do you think he's the murderer?" asked Mrs Morrell.

"He's certainly suspicious," he replied, "as is Billy Kemery. We'll need to work quickly now. We can't have anyone escaping justice."

"Just one quick request before I leave," said Augusta. "Can I take look at Miss Taylor's diaries, please?"

"Of course. We haven't found anything terribly interesting in them, but by all means have a look for yourself, Mrs Peel. All she really did was keep a record of appointments. Nothing's been written down in any detail, I'm afraid."

Gabriel Lennox watched from the riverside wall as Augusta stepped out through the gates of Scotland Yard and walked toward the bus stop. "Still sniffing about," he muttered to himself. "She'll stop at nothing to impress that old spy friend of hers."

He turned up the collar of his coat and followed her.

Chapter 44

As THE BUS proceeded along Victoria Embankment, Augusta looked at Jean Taylor's diaries. Detective Inspector Fisher had given her 1919, 1920 and 1921 to peruse. They were small, with a whole week printed on each page. The space for each day was only just large enough to accommodate a few notes.

She felt a twinge of sadness as she turned to look at the entry for the day of Miss Taylor's death. The lack of notes after that day emphasised the fact that her life had been cut short. With a lump in her throat, she began to examine the entries. It wasn't long before she found Gabriel's name written down. She found it a second time, then a third. The pair appeared to have met quite regularly before Jean's death. She took her notebook out of her handbag and began to make notes.

Augusta hopped off the bus at High Holborn and made her way toward Holborn Library. Sharing its premises with the town hall, the library was an attractive cream building with carved stone decorations.

"Augusta!" whispered Dorothy Jones at the front desk. "How nice to see you. Have you finished repairing those books?"

"Almost." Noticing Dorothy's disappointed expression, she added, "I've been quite busy."

"You're just here to browse, then?"

"Sort of. Can you show me where you keep old newspapers?"

"Of course. We only have the last three years' worth available on this floor. If you want anything older than that, we'll have to get them out of storage."

"I'm interested in the ones from about a month ago."

"Oh. Why's that, then?"

"I just need to jog my memory about something."

"I'll show you where they are."

Augusta followed her to the back of the library.

"I must say I'm relieved to hear that Harriet wants nothing more to do with that awful Mr Lennox," whispered the girl's mother.

"She told you that?"

"Yes. I asked her about him, of course, as I was terribly worried she was still fond of him. She told me she had quite forgotten about him."

Augusta did her best to hide her puzzled expression. Presumably Harriet wanted to ensure that her mother heard nothing of her plans to travel to Paris with Mr Lennox. *Poor, oblivious Dorothy. Should I tell her?* Augusta was tempted for a moment, but thought better of it. It would send Dorothy into a spin and then all hell would break loose.

Better to keep it quiet for now. Hopefully the police will get to Gabriel before he manages to escape.

. . .

It was dusk by the time Augusta began her fifteen-minute walk home, and a light fog was settling in. She had gathered some useful information, but everything had been overshadowed by the news of Laurence Costello's death. He had initially seemed suspicious, but it was hard for Augusta to believe that he had murdered Jean Taylor. Judging by Florence Morrell's fondness for him, he was largely a good man who had fallen in with some extremely unpleasant people.

The streets were reasonably busy until she turned into Bernard Street by the Russell Hotel. The fog had thickened along the way, and by the time Augusta reached Marchmont Street she could see very little around her. She didn't usually feel nervous walking along the road where she lived, but something about the fog and the eerie quietness unnerved her. A prickle ran up the back of her neck.

The grocer's shop was just about visible in the gloom. It had closed its doors early for the evening and a dim light was visible at the back of the shop. Only twenty yards remained between Augusta and her home.

As she passed the grocer's van, a quick movement caught her eye. She glanced around but saw nothing further. Sensing someone was up to no good, she quickened her step.

The sound of a scuffed footfall from behind made her spin around.

There was a shadowy figure about three yards away from her, and it appeared to be moving closer.

A shot split the air and the hazy figure crumpled to the ground. Augusta let out a cry. She wanted to run to the injured person, but fear of another shot being fired stopped her in her tracks.

More footsteps sounded in the road and another figure appeared. It bent over the form on the ground, which moaned in pain.

Augusta found the courage to run over. As she did so, the bent figure stood up straight.

"Are you all right, Mrs Peel?"

"Jacques?"

The figure on the ground moaned again. Augusta saw something next to him and peered closer.

A cricket bat.

Was it intended for me?

The man on the ground cried out in anguish as he pulled himself up into a sitting position. Blood pooled around his foot.

"He needs a tourniquet," said Jacques, swiftly removing his tie.

"Gabriel?" she said, still staring at the man.

Gabriel looked down, avoiding her gaze.

"He was about to hit you," said Jacques, pulling his tie tight around Gabriel's leg. He yelped in pain. "I had to stop him. He might have killed you!"

"Thank you." She struggled to think what else to say. *Had Gabriel intended to murder me?* Perhaps it was to be expected from a man who had shot his former fiancée. "I'll call for an ambulance," she said.

A sash window slid open above their heads.

"What happened?" came a voice.

"Are you on the telephone?" Augusta called up.

"Yes, shall I call for the police?"

"Call an ambulance!"

A rotund man emerged from the grocer's. "What's going on?"

"Just an accident," said Augusta. "Someone's tele-phoning for help."

"Call the police, too," muttered Gabriel. "Tell them what everyone's been waiting to hear. I confess to Jean Taylor's murder. I did it! I shot her!"

Chapter 45

"How you are feeling, Mrs Peel?" asked Detective Inspector Fisher. "Is the tea all right?"

"The tea's very good, thank you."

"Excellent. It's the one redeeming feature of this gloomy place." He glanced around the little room inside Hunter Street police station. "Rumour has it the Victorians built this station because they didn't know what else to put here. Troublesome residents, apparently. They kept pulling the houses down and rebuilding them, but the problems persisted until the police station was built."

"Is there any word on Mr Lennox's condition?"

"Not yet. Two men from E Division are with him at University College Hospital. Unpleasant business. He'll have lost a fair bit of blood, too. I think it's safe to say that Jacques saved you from serious injury. He possibly even saved your life."

"I presume he was waiting outside my flat in another attempt to speak to me. I'm lucky that he persevered."

"Very lucky." He reached out and patted her hand. "I'm glad you're all right, Mrs Peel. It's all turned out rather well, especially if we manage to get a full confession from Mr Lennox. In the meantime, E Division will need a statement from you about what happened."

"It was all over in a matter of seconds."

"So I understand. Jacques's with them now. He told me he wants to speak to us both."

She sighed. "Why? Nothing we say can change what happened. None of us can bring Sarah back."

"I feel the same way. But perhaps he just wants to be listened to. Sometimes it helps people if they're given the chance to explain."

"Before we get into any of that, your men need to find Harriet Jones. She lives near here with her mother, Dorothy. The address is Cartwright Gardens, number seventeen."

He made a note of this. "May I ask why?"

"I think she knows more than she's letting on."

There was a knock at the door and Jacques stepped in. "I am sorry to interrupt, but it is important for me to speak to you both. Please, just a few minutes of your time and then I will leave you alone."

Detective Inspector Fisher glanced at Augusta and she gave a reluctant nod. She couldn't face a confrontation, but Jacques had saved her life. The least she could do was listen to what he had to say.

The Frenchman sat down and took a deep breath.

Chapter 46

THE DAMP AIR cooled Augusta's face as she stepped outside the police station. She was standing in a yard surrounded by tall, shabby buildings. The fog had enveloped them all, leaving just a few faint lights glimmering from the windows nearby.

"Mrs Peel?" came Detective Inspector Fisher's voice.

"Over here." Augusta mopped at her eyes with her handkerchief, then quickly shoved it into her pocket before he joined her.

"That was a lot to take in," he said.

"It certainly was. Jacques mustn't bear all the responsibility for Sarah's capture, though. We were all to blame in one way or another."

"I agree. But it seems that's what he wants, and I suppose we've done our bit by accepting what he had to say. He's just as upset as we are, and that's the way he's chosen to deal with it."

"By travelling across the Channel and following us around until we agreed to talk to him?"

"Yes. He always was a rather serious, determined fellow, wasn't he?"

"Indeed," she agreed. "Still, it was easier talking about it than I imagined it would be."

"I felt the same way."

"I'm not sure why I resisted it for so long."

"Because neither of us wanted to bring all those things up again. At least, we didn't relish the thought of doing so. He rather forced it on us, but I don't suppose that was such a bad thing." He gave her arm a gentle squeeze. "Come on, let's get back inside. I've just asked E Division to send a man to track down Harriet Jones. You didn't get a chance to explain why we need to find her, but I trust your instincts. How about another cup of tea before he brings her in?"

Augusta nodded. "I'd like that."

Chapter 47

A SHORT WHILE LATER, a young constable stepped into the interview room where Detective Inspector Fisher and Augusta were awaiting the arrival of Harriet. He was out of breath, clearly having run back to the station.

"No sign of her, sir," he puffed. "She's scarpered."

"What?" The senior officer got to his feet. "Does anyone have any idea where she went?"

"Her mother had no idea at all. She thought the girl was in her bedroom, but when she went up there, she saw that Miss Jones's things were missing. I've just spoken to a man who recently passed a young woman carrying a trunk, sir. Headed north, she was. St Pancras and King's Cross train stations are both up that way."

"How long ago was that?"

"Ten minutes or so, sir. Perhaps even fifteen."

"She can't be moving terribly swiftly if she has a trunk with her."

"Unless she jumped in a taxi cab, sir."

"You're right! She'll be able to flag one down on Euston Road easily enough. Quick, get after her!" He turned to Augusta. "I'll speak to the superintendent and ask him to coordinate a search."

"She may already have reached one of the stations."

"Yes, I realise that."

Augusta sighed. This was exactly what she had wanted to avoid. Harriet must have heard about the shot fired just a few streets from her home. Perhaps Gabriel had even managed to get a message to her. Either way, she had obviously fled, and now it might be too late to find her.

She took another sip of tea, then put her cup down. It was no use her sitting around doing nothing.

Harriet has to be found.

Augusta put on her coat, picked up her handbag and prepared to leave.

Detective Inspector Fisher caught her just before she reached the station door. "Are you heading home?"

"No. I'm off to find Harriet Jones!"

"I think you should go home and rest. You've had an eventful evening."

"Nonsense! I'm going to King's Cross station."

"Why there?"

"I remember her telling me about an aunt in York. She's very fond of this aunt, so perhaps that's where she's heading. Trains for York depart from King's Cross, don't they?"

"I believe so. Euston serves the North West and St Pancras serves the Midlands. It must be King's Cross for York."

"Good. I'll get going, then." She stepped out of the door.

"Wait!" He hobbled after her. "I'll come with you!"

She pointed at his stick. "Can you run with that thing?"

"Not really, no. I'll get someone to drive us."

"By the time we get in a car, I could just as easily have gone by foot. I'll leave now and meet you there."

Before he could argue, Augusta had jogged off along Judd Street. The long row of railings on the left helped her navigate through the fog up to Euston Road. As she turned right, she was just able to make out the glimmer of lights from the imposing Midland Grand Hotel, which stood across the road. She fervently hoped any passing vehicles had their lights on as she crossed over. Once she was back on the pavement, she ran as quickly as the limited visibility allowed.

Did Harriet really come this way? It was possible that she had hailed a taxi and gone in a completely different direction. There was no knowing for sure, so Augusta simply had to follow her hunch and do her best to find the girl.

A series of advertising hoardings loomed out of the gloom. She had to be close to the station now.

"Have you seen a young woman pass by here?" she asked a man standing beside a van. "Carrying a trunk?" She couldn't imagine many young women travelling alone in the evening.

He shrugged. "Dunno. Might've."

"Thanks for your help."

She hurried into the station, where the fog had managed to find its way up into the arches of the wrought-iron roof. She recalled from previous visits here that there were six platforms. Three trains sat beside the buffers. *Are any of them heading to York this evening?*

A young woman with a trunk was unlikely to stand out among the countless groups of passengers making their way around the station. Augusta looked around. *What colour is Harriet's overcoat?* She felt sure it was brown. But it seemed as though just about every woman around her was wearing a brown coat.

She called out to a porter pulling a trolley piled high with luggage and asked him where the next train to York would be departing from.

"Platform four."

So there is an imminent departure.

"Is this the train to York?" she asked a couple as they jogged along platform four. "Newcastle," replied the man, "but I think it stops at York. You'd better be quick, though. It leaves in two minutes!"

Augusta ran along behind them, peering in through the windows in the hope of catching a glimpse of Harriet. Then, just up ahead, she saw a young woman in a brown coat with dark, bobbed hair trying to lift a trunk onto the train.

"Stop!" she cried out, running up behind her.

The girl cried out as Augusta grabbed her arm. She felt a sickening twist in her stomach as the girl turned. It wasn't Harriet.

"I'm so sorry. I thought you were someone else."

"That's how you treat your friends, is it?" snapped the woman.

Augusta apologised again, then looked up and down the train once more. If Harriet had boarded there was no chance of finding her now.

The guard's whistle blew.

Perhaps Harriet isn't on the train after all. Maybe it was nothing but a foolish notion.

The whistle blew again and the engine let out a great plume of steam and smoke as it prepared to pull away. The carriages gave a jolt and began to edge forward.

A window slid down in the next carriage along from where Augusta stood, and a young woman's face peered out. Her expression was wide-eyed at first, but then it turned to mirth.

Harriet Jones.

"Harriet!" shouted Augusta. "Get off the train!" She moved to catch up with the carriage, but the train had begun to move a little faster. "Get off!"

Harriet laughed, her dark hair billowing around her face as the train picked up speed.

Augusta felt a bitter taste in her mouth. "They'll get you!" she shouted out. "You can't run forever!"

The smile left Harriet's face and her eyes widened once again. Something on the platform had alarmed her.

Augusta stopped running and turned to see a group of blue-uniformed police officers running toward her. She heard shouting from further down the platform.

Another whistle blew and the carriages began to judder. A dreadful screech sounded.

Augusta smiled. The train was coming to a stop.

The officers ran past her toward Harriet's carriage. Shunting and groaning, the train ground to a halt.

At the far end of the platform Augusta saw a man leaning on a stick, remonstrating with the man in the guard's van.

Detective Inspector Fisher's here and Harriet's time is up.

Chapter 48

"WHY HAVE YOU BROUGHT ME HERE?" protested Harriet Jones, seated between two constables in the interview room at Hunter Street station. "I've done nothing wrong!"

"Why were you running away, then?" asked Detective Inspector Fisher.

"I wasn't! I was on my way to visit Auntie Dora."

"Did she know you were on your way?"

"It was to be a surprise!"

"An interesting time to spring a surprise, wouldn't you say? Late on a foggy October evening. That train wouldn't have reached York much before eleven o'clock. And besides, you'd have been expected at work tomorrow morning. A sewing mistress, aren't you?"

Harriet said nothing and looked away.

He gave Augusta an encouraging nod. "I suppose we'd better hear from you, Mrs Peel. Why *is* Miss Jones here?"

Augusta took her notebook out of her handbag. She wasn't enjoying this moment at all. Harriet Jones had been like a niece to her. What she was about to say would seem like a huge betrayal. Then again, Harriet had gone to great lengths to deceive her.

"I recalled Dorothy Jones, Harriet's mother, telling me her daughter had witnessed an accident a few weeks ago," she said. "Lord Shellbrook crashed his car into the statue of Eros in Piccadilly Circus, apparently."

"I remember it well," he responded.

"I wondered at the time what Harriet was doing there so early in the morning, especially as her usual routine was to walk from her home in Cartwright Gardens to the school where she works on Old Gloucester Street. The distance is just over half a mile, and Piccadilly Circus would have been quite a detour. I've walked it myself, and it's easily a three-mile round trip."

"Quite a detour indeed."

"When I learned that Mr Gabriel Lennox lived on Glasshouse Street – a road that leads to Piccadilly Circus – I realised why Miss Jones might have been there that morning. My first thought was that she had stayed overnight at his flat and was walking to work when she witnessed the accident. But I couldn't imagine her staying there because Mrs Jones would never have allowed her daughter to stay out all night.

"So what was Miss Jones doing so close to Mr Lennox's flat that morning? This was where Miss Taylor's diary came in handy, because she'd recorded all her meetings with Mr Lennox. Several evening meetings were marked in her diary. I made a note of these dates, then looked up the date of Lord Shellbrook's accident. I found it in a copy of the *Evening Standard* at Holborn Library. The date of the crash was Friday the thirtieth of September. According to Miss Taylor's diary, she had spent the previous evening with Mr Lennox. Could she have stayed at his flat that night? I suspected she had.

"I don't know why Miss Jones decided to visit the locality the following morning. Perhaps she suspected that Mr Lennox was seeing another woman or perhaps she regularly kept an eye on his flat. Either way, I believe she saw Miss Taylor leaving that morning."

Detective Inspector Fisher turned to Harriet. "Is that so?"

She shrugged.

"She isn't denying it," he said.

"I can't prove it just yet," continued Augusta, "but perhaps Miss Jones watched Mr Lennox's flat on a number of occasions and had regularly witnessed Miss Taylor visiting and leaving. If that's the case, she knew full well who Miss Taylor was and suspected the relationship between her and Mr Lennox was ongoing in some shape or form."

"Interesting," he said, consulting his notebook. "On the seventeenth of October you brought Miss Jones to us with a letter from Mr Lennox explaining that he had once been engaged to Miss Taylor. Miss Jones had no knowledge of the engagement up to that point."

"Well, that's what she claimed. I think the letter was written in a deliberate attempt to mislead us. The one thing Miss Jones and Mr Lennox wanted to do was demonstrate that she had no knowledge of the affair."

"But why?"

"Because Harriet Jones shot Miss Taylor."

The girl clasped her face in her hands.

"But Mr Lennox has confessed to the crime," said the detective inspector.

"He adores this girl so much he'd do anything to protect her."

His brow furrowed. "If that's the case, Mrs Peel, how do you suppose the events of that evening unravelled?"

"Well, to begin with, I don't think Miss Jones went to Flo's Club intending to commit murder."

"Are you saying it was an accident?"

"I think it was a situation that got out of hand."

"Clearly."

"Am I right in thinking you have a witness who claims to have seen Mr Lennox speaking with Miss Taylor, Detective Inspector?"

"That's correct."

"It's possible that the pair wanted to continue their conversation somewhere private and chose to meet up in the storage room. Mr Lennox will hopefully confirm that as soon as he's well enough to be interviewed. So they went up to the storage room and Miss Jones, feeling suspicious and upset, followed them."

"Without them noticing?"

"It's possible."

"Did you follow them up there, Miss Jones?"

The girl looked down and wiped her eyes.

"So you're suggesting, Mrs Peel, that Miss Jones tailed the pair into the storage room and then confronted them?"

"Yes. Then the confrontation descended into a physical altercation. A struggle broke out and someone knocked into the shelving, causing various items to fall off the shelves."

"Including the box of menu cards Mr Costello had hidden Mr Kemery's revolver in!"

"That's right."

"And that's when Miss Jones seized the gun and shot Miss Taylor with it?"

"Yes, I think that's what must have happened. Only I'm not sure Mr Lennox was still there at that stage. I think he would have broken up the fight had he been present."

"Where had he gone?"

"I think a better explanation would be that Miss Jones was watching the storage room from somewhere nearby. When I visited the storage room, I noticed a long pair of curtains in front of the window on the landing. Miss Jones could have hidden herself behind those. Perhaps she hadn't planned to confront Miss Taylor but decided to do so when she saw Mr Lennox leave."

"Why did he leave the room alone, do you think?"

"The pair didn't want to be seen leaving together, did they? They had met in secret. And if Mr Lennox is to be believed, the conversation may have been about ending their affair. He claims he was keen to concentrate on his new relationship with Miss Jones. Perhaps he was trying to put an end to things with Miss Taylor once and for all. If so, Miss Taylor would have been rather upset and may have wanted to remain in the storage room to allow any redness around her eyes to subside."

"You're suggesting, then, that once Mr Lennox left the storage room, Miss Jones went in and confronted Miss Taylor?"

"Yes. At that point the confrontation became physical and the situation escalated. Perhaps Miss Taylor pushed Miss Jones against the shelving. Someone certainly knocked into the shelves at some point because the box containing the gun was knocked to the ground. Perhaps they both dived for the gun when it fell out, each fearful that the other would get there first. I can only guess that Miss Jones won."

"A tussle is one thing," said Detective Inspector Fisher, "but firing a fatal shot… that's quite another, wouldn't you say?"

"Yes, especially if it was premeditated. But maybe it

was self-defence or a response to provocation in this case. Emotions were running high and alcohol had been consumed. You didn't mean to kill her, did you, Harriet?"

The girl let out an enormous sob. "No!"

Chapter 49

"So what happened after that, Miss Jones?" asked Detective Inspector Fisher. "Where did you hide the gun?"

There was a pause as the girl seemed to consider whether there was any use in lying.

"I don't know what happened to it," she said with a sigh. "I threw it onto the floor and that's the last I saw of it. I couldn't believe what I'd done. I just panicked! I opened the door to find Mr Costello standing there."

"He was on the other side of the door?"

"He'd just come up the stairs. I was so scared. I knew I was in big trouble... I could hardly breathe! I told him he couldn't go inside the room, and that he had to go and fetch Gabe." She paused to wipe her eyes. "They both came back a moment later. Gabe asked me what had happened and I said there'd been an accident. He told me to go downstairs and they would see to it."

"So he knew Miss Taylor was dead."

"No, none of us knew she was dead at that point. I hoped she wasn't, but I just didn't know. It was so horrible! And the gunshot was so loud I was half-deaf for a while.

Then when I went downstairs the police came rushing in! I thought they were there for me, so I dashed away to the cloakroom. I hid there for a bit, then once I was calm I pretended nothing had happened. That was all I could do! I can't tell you how relieved I was when you got me out of there, Mrs Peel."

"So Mr Lennox and Mr Costello tidied up the murder scene?" asked the detective inspector.

"Yes. Gabe told me they wiped everything for finger-prints and tidied the bits that had fallen off the shelves. They had to leave her where she was, though. There was nothing else they could do with the police running around the building."

"I'm amazed her body wasn't discovered during the raid," he said. "They obviously didn't check the storage room, and Costello didn't make it known for an hour or two. We took him at his word."

"So he was dragged into it," said Augusta. "He knew what had happened but chose to protect you, Harriet."

"So did Gabe."

"Presumably it was Mr Costello who took the gun," said Detective Inspector Fisher. "And managed to sneak it out of there. My colleagues would have searched everyone for weapons during the raid but they missed Mrs Morrell's assistant."

"And presumably it was Mr Costello who then planted the gun in Cissy Drummond's dressing room," added Augusta.

"Anything to avoid the eye of suspicion from settling on Miss Jones here."

Augusta shook her head. "All those lies you told after-wards, Harriet. They make you the best actress of the lot."

"I didn't intend to lie. I had no choice!"

"You conspired with Gabriel to write the letter that

supposedly informed you of his former engagement to Miss Taylor."

"*You* asked him to write it, Mrs Peel!"

"You're right, I did. At that stage I thought you were an innocent young woman. You were so convincing! There was one thing you didn't lie about, and that was Mr Lennox's innocence. You were certain he was innocent because you *knew* he was."

"But why would he cover up for Miss Jones?" asked Detective Inspector Fisher. "Why would he care so much about Miss Jones if he was still seeing his former fiancée? Why confess to a murder he didn't commit?"

"That's something you'd need to ask him," replied Augusta. "There's no doubt he's very taken with Miss Jones. I can only imagine that when he came across that awful scene in the storage room his instinct was to cover it up and protect her. He probably regrets it now."

"No, he doesn't!" snapped Harriet. "He wanted us to be together! Why else would he ask me to go to Paris with him?"

"To help you evade justice. Do you really believe he wanted to marry you?"

"Yes!"

The detective inspector shook his head, seemingly trying to comprehend the turn of events. "Miss Jones has always struck me as a pleasant young lady, Mrs Peel. What on earth made you suspect her?"

"I didn't suspect her for some time; she had me completely fooled. But then I began to wonder why she had such unwavering confidence in Gabriel Lennox's innocence. Surely any girl, no matter how naive, would at least consider for a moment that he might have been guilty. And then there was all that talk of dashing off to Paris with him after convincing her mother that she wanted nothing more to do with the man. I realised then what a good liar she was.

"When I considered that she could have been consistently lying to me I began to question everything she'd said. There were little signs that made me realise she and Mr Lennox had probably been communicating all along. He called at my flat one evening, upset that Miss Jones had spoken to you, Detective Inspector. He told me the police had informed him about the interview, but I realised he had more likely heard it from Miss Jones, because you usually don't like to be too open about your investigations with suspects. Am I right?"

He nodded.

"And I see now that it was no great coincidence that Mr Lennox tried to attack me shortly after I'd told Miss Jones I was close to proving that Gabriel was behind the framing of Cissy Drummond and the theft of Lady Hereford's canary. The two were conversing more often than we realised."

"I suppose we just need Mr Lennox to confirm his side of the story now," said Detective Inspector Fisher.

"I want to see him!" cried Harriet.

"I don't know about that," he replied. "He'll be facing serious charges himself. He helped cover up a murder and planned to carry out a brutal attack on Mrs Peel. What a lovely pair the two of you make!"

There was a knock at the door and the desk sergeant stepped in. "Mrs Jones is here," he said. "She'd like to see her daughter."

The senior officer nodded.

"If it's all right with you, Detective Inspector," said Augusta, "I'll make myself scarce before she's shown in."

Chapter 50

CISSY DRUMMOND's black Crossley Landaulette pulled up outside the house with the white gate in Hampstead Garden Suburb. The actress climbed out and made her way to the front door, her head bowed. Her driver followed, carrying several pieces of luggage.

"Edith!" Cissy's mother gave her a strong embrace once she was inside. "It's so nice to have you home again. They'll leave you alone here."

"I hope so, Ma."

William's form was blurred by her tears as he ran up to her. "I've made an aeroplane!"

She smiled and wiped her eyes. "Then you must show it to me!" Seeing him again helped push all the recent unpleasantness to the back of her mind.

As she followed him into the front room, she heard the driver address her mother in the hallway. "Where shall I put Miss Drummond's bags, madam?"

"Her name is Miss *Parkinson*. Take them upstairs, please. Second room on the left."

Edith smiled as she made herself comfortable on the rug with her son.

Cissy Drummond was no more.

Chapter 51

"So THIS IS where you spend your time," said Detective Inspector Fisher, glancing around Augusta's workshop. "Is that a tube train I can hear?"

"Yes. The Piccadilly line."

"Gosh, that must get on your nerves."

"Actually, it doesn't. I find it rather soothing."

"Do you?" He listened a short while longer. "I suppose I can understand that… no, actually I can't. It would try my patience after a while."

She glanced at the book in his hand. "Is that the one you want me to repair, Detective Inspector Fisher?"

"*Mr* Fisher, please. No need to be long-winded about it. Yes, this is the one." He handed it to her.

The book was bound in red cloth and had the silhouettes of five children on the cover. *The Adventures of Huckleberry Finn* was written across it in gold lettering.

"I imagine you were expecting something more grown-up and highbrow from me," he added, "but it's always been my favourite. Even after all these years."

"There's nothing wrong with that. It's one that I love,

too. And it's not in bad condition."

"Remarkable condition, I'd say, considering the travails I put it through during my boyhood. But some of the pages have come loose and the cover is threatening to detach itself."

"It'll be easy to repair. And now's a good time to do it, before it gets any worse."

"Wonderful. How's Sparky?"

"Very well, thank you. Singing as if nothing ever happened to him."

"What a stoic little chap. Any word on when Lady Hereford will be back to retrieve him?"

"No, I'm hoping it'll be a while yet. I know he's only a bird, but I enjoy his company."

"I know what you mean. I feel the same way about my dachshund, Herbert. Not that he does anything I tell him to, mind you, but he has character. By the way, you might like to know that Harriet Jones and Gabriel Lennox are due to appear before the magistrates tomorrow morning."

"That's good. Mr Lennox is recovered, then?"

"He seems to be. I think the bullet wound was fairly superficial in the end. Jacques fired the perfect disabling shot."

"He was always rather good at that, wasn't he?"

"Indeed he was."

Augusta thought about Harriet facing the magistrates. She wouldn't cope with it well, but it was the price she would have to pay. "I can't imagine what it must be like for Harriet's mother, Dorothy, at the moment."

"Have you seen her?"

"No, I don't think she wants anything to do with me. I suspect she holds me partly responsible for what's happened."

He laughed. "I suppose it helps some people to have

someone to blame when awful things happen. It's rather foolish, all the same. Thank you for your help with the Jean Taylor case. If it hadn't been for your involvement, an actress would have been unfairly convicted of murder and the dreadful duo would be living a wonderful new life in Paris."

"I'm sure you'd have reached the same conclusion without me."

"I don't think I would have, actually. I'm not sure I ever would have suspected Miss Jones. Just goes to show the power of a pretty face, doesn't it?"

"I'm sure you can see beyond that."

"Not as well as you, Mrs Peel. Anyway, I'd better be on my way." He surveyed the room again, as if reluctant to leave. "Nice to see your workshop. Do let me know how much I owe you."

"What for?"

"For repairing the book."

"Nonsense, there's no charge for that."

"You can't do it for nothing!"

"It's a favour. For a friend."

"A friend?" Even in the gloom of her workshop, she noticed a little colour appear in his cheeks. "Right, well, erm, that's very kind of you, Mrs Peel."

"*Augusta*, please. No need to be long-winded about it."

He raised an eyebrow. "In which case, you'd better call me Philip."

"Is that your real name?"

He laughed. "After all we went through during the war, you should know that I couldn't possibly say. What about Augusta?"

"My real name?"

"Well, is it?"

"I couldn't possibly say!"

The End

Thank you

≈

Thank you for reading *Death in Soho* I really hope you
enjoyed it!

Would you like to know when I release new books? Here
are some ways to stay updated:

- Join my mailing list and receive an extra
  chapter from *Death in Soho*:
  emilyorgan.com/augusta-peel-sign-up
- Like my Facebook page: facebook.com/
  emilyorganwriter
- Follow me on Goodreads:
  goodreads.com/emily_organ
- Follow me on BookBub: bookbub.com/au-
  thors/emily-organ
- View my other books here: emilyorgan.com

And if you have a moment, I would be very grateful if you would leave a quick review of *Death in Soho* online. Honest reviews of my books help other readers discover them too!

Historical Note

The inspiration for Florence Morrell is Kate Meyrick, otherwise known in her time as the 'Night Club Queen'. Born in Ireland, she had eight children with her husband before their separation. She then embarked on a career as a London nightclub owner and her famous 43 Club on Gerrard Street, Soho, was the haunt of royalty, aristocracy and celebrities of the day. Regulars included Rudolf Valentino, Tallulah Bankhead, JB Priestly and Evelyn Waugh. Meyrick was the inspiration behind the character Ma Mayfield in Waugh's classic novel *Brideshead Revisited*.

During the First World War, strict alcohol licensing laws were enforced in Britain and these remained in place during the 1920s. The restriction of alcohol didn't fit well with the hedonistic Jazz Age and many night time venues sold alcohol in secret. Kate Meyrick was fined multiple times for selling alcohol outside of licensing hours and served four prison sentences. Each time her club was closed down, she reopened it under a new name – a legal loophole which frustrated the authorities.

The 1920s saw increased public concern about the use

of recreational drugs. High profile deaths from drugs over-doses included Billie Carleton, an actress who died of a cocaine overdose at the Savoy Hotel after attending the Victory Ball to celebrate the end of the First World War at the Royal Albert Hall in November 1918. Another death which shocked the nation was that of Freda Kempton, a dancer who overdosed on cocaine supplied by notorious Chinese drug dealer Brilliant Chang in 1922. Such inci-dents made the Metropolitan Police and the Home Secre-tary, William Joynson-Hicks, determined to crack down on London's nightlife. The relationship between the authori-ties and London's night club owners became a game of cat and mouse.

Police raids on night clubs were common. Undercover police officers were routinely sent into clubs to observe the selling of alcohol out of hours. As this work involved buying and drinking alcohol themselves, this can't have been a difficult job for them! Blue Branch was an under-cover police unit set up to do just this. In 1927, a member of Blue Branch - Sergeant George Goddard - was found guilty of accepting bribes from Kate Meyrick in return for not reporting her breaches of licensing laws. Kate Meyrick served all her prison sentences at Holloway Prison. The final two sentences were for hard labour which took a toll on her health. She died in 1933 at the age of 57.

The theatres featured in this story are fictional as is Flo's Club (which is based on the 43 Club). Marchmont Street, where Augusta Peel lives, is a small shopping street in Bloomsbury. It was built in the nineteenth century and London Underground's Piccadilly Line runs beneath it on the route between Russell Square and King's Cross. The British actor and comedian Kenneth Williams lived on the street for many years.

Vine Street police station is said to have once been the busiest police station in the world, probably due to its location in the heart of London's West End between Regent Street and Piccadilly. It operated from 1829 until 1940 and then again from 1971 until 1997. The building was demolished in 2005.

Hunter Street police station was built in Bloomsbury in the early twentieth century on a site which had housed troublesome residents during the nineteenth century. After repeated redevelopment and bouts of criminal behaviour, it was thought a police station would solve the problem. The building now houses students.

Get an extra chapter!

~

Want more of Augusta Peel? Sign up to my mailing list and I'll send you an extra chapter from *Death in Soho*!

Augusta Peel pays a visit to Lady Hereford in hospital. Should she tell her about Sparky's kidnap or pretend that everything has been just fine?

Visit my website for more details:

emilyorgan.com/augusta-peel-sign-up

Or scan this QR code with a mobile device:

Murder in the Air

An Augusta Peel Mystery Book 2

Is airship travel safe? Not if there's a killer on board.

When business magnate Robert Jeffreys announces his investment in airships, he hosts a promotional flight for a group of reporters. Working undercover in the crew is retired spy Augusta Peel. She'd rather be working on her book repair business but Inspector Fisher of Scotland Yard has persuaded her to help with a surveillance operation.

The press trip on the airship takes a turn when a body is found in a cabin. Augusta now has a new challenge on her hands. Can she identify the murderer? It's tricky to find a motive among the sophisticated passengers – some of them are sophisticated liars too.

Events escalate when a second death occurs. The airship murderer is covering their tracks. Augusta faces a race against time before the culprit tracks her down and silences her too.

Find out more here: emilyorgan.com/murder-air

The Penny Green Series

Also by Emily Organ. Escape to 1880s London! A page-turning historical mystery series.

As one of the first female reporters on 1880s Fleet Street, plucky Penny Green has her work cut out. Whether it's investigating the mysterious death of a friend or reporting on a serial killer in the slums, Penny must rely on her wits and determination to discover the truth.

Fortunately she can rely on the help of Inspector James Blakely of Scotland Yard, but will their relationship remain professional?

Find out more here: emilyorgan.com/penny-green-victorian-mystery-series

The Churchill & Pemberley Series

Also by Emily Organ. Join senior sleuths Churchill and Pemberley as they tackle cake and crime in an English village.

Growing bored in the autumn of her years, Londoner Annabel Churchill buys a private detective agency in a Dorset village. The purchase brings with it the eccentric Doris Pemberley and the two ladies are soon solving mysteries and chasing down miscreants in sleepy Compton Poppleford.

Plenty of characters are out to scupper their chances, among them grumpy Inspector Mappin. Another challenge is their four-legged friend who means well but has a problem with discipline.

But the biggest challenge is one which threatens to derail every case they work on: will there be enough tea and cake?

Find out more here: emilyorgan.com/the-churchill-pemberley-cozy-mystery-series